Kalista's Hope

By Kara S. McKenzie

Light Romance Quaint Books
http://karasmckenzie.weebly.com

ISBN-13: 978-1515053415
ISBN-10: 1515053415

Cover Photo Copyright © 2015 by Kara S. McKenzie. All rights reserved.
Use with permission.

Cover design by Janielescueta of Fiverr.

Copyright © 2015 by Kara S. McKenzie.
Printed by Createspace, An Amazon.com Company

All rights reserved. This is a work of fiction. The characters, names,
incidents, places, and dialogue are either products of the author's
imagination, and are not to be construed as real or are used fictitiously. No
part of this book may be reproduced in any format or in any medium
without the written permission of the author.

Acknowledgements

I want to thank both my family and friends in their continued support of my book. I cannot name all of those who encouraged me in so many different ways, by reading my books; giving suggestions and helping me realize my potential. Those included are my immediate family, my extended family, my Bible study group, my school friends, my on-line writer buddies, and both my Cedarville, Climax and Scotts hometown friends. I truly appreciate all the loving support shown.

Dedication

To the lunch bunch…

Kalista's Hope

By Kara S. McKenzie

Chapter 1

Kalista hesitated beneath the arched marble doorway to the room sculpted in a typical Roman design. Her eyes followed the deep lines of the Corinthian columns on each side of her, cold, hard and unbending, like tall armored warriors standing at attention. The stark white walls surrounding her seemed ready to swallow her up as she entered the massive room set aside for meals. She tapped her fingers on her side, reticent to go further.

She reached up and brushed a strand of hair out of her eyes and adjusted the tilted wreath of tiny white flowers that encircled her head. As it kept tipping to the side, she wondered why she bothered with it. The thing never stayed on.

It really didn't matter, anyway. Domnica was the only one who really cared how she looked, and that was only for appearance's sake for others. And what that woman thought made no difference to Kalista. She was tired of her stepmother's games and ridiculous comments.

She took a step, holding the edge of her gown in her hand and then lifted her chin, smiling. If Domnica only knew, her feet, which were hidden beneath the heavy folds of fabric of her gown were bare, she'd be furious. But, what did it matter? Domnica wasn't her mother and had no right to tell her what to do.

She tightened the golden ribbon clasped loosely about her waist. Her eyes narrowed as she looked across the room. She reluctantly made her way to the long table in front of the window and braced herself for yet another vexing encounter with this tiresome woman and her daughter.

The slaves in the room paid little attention to her as she walked past them, barely moving out of her way. They were too busy to bother with the likes of her, worried more about pleasing the petty whims of Domnica and Camila.

Her stepmother leaned against the slanted headrest of a seat, padded with silk. She lifted a goblet of wine to her lips and took a sip.

When she spotted Kalista making her way toward the table, she put down the drink in her hand. "She's finally up. You'd think she'd check the sundial." Domnica turned to Camila.

Kalista's stepsister slid her fingers between strands of dark blonde hair that had fallen neatly over her heavily jeweled tunic. She played with the silken ends. "Kalista? No one in Rome could get her to do her that." She laughed.

Domnica smiled catlike. "Come, Kalista. What have you done with your hair?"

Kalista wrapped a fiery curl around her finger, debating whether she wanted to sit down. If it weren't for her father, she wouldn't have even been there. She spoke quietly. "Why do you care, if I don't?" The room fell silent, the slaves slinking back into the corners of the room.

Domnica lifted the chalice of purple wine to her lips again and took another sip, setting it back down on the table next to her. "It'll matter to your father."

Kalista dug her nails deeply into the folds of her rumpled gown. She turned when one of the older slave women dressed in a simple brown tunic, with a wooden tray laden with food, hobbled into the room.

"Nona!" Domnica clapped her hands.

The woman scurried over the patterned tiles to her mistress's side. She set the platter filled with delicacies of fruits, nuts, and bread on the table and bowed. Her hands trembled. "Yes?"

Domnica got up, towering over her. "Tell Kalista's father I need to speak with him...about her, again." She pointed a long, thin finger in the direction of the young woman standing beside her.

Nona bowed. "Yes, mistress." She shot an anxious glance at Kalista, then lifted the edge of her skirt and limped awkwardly in the direction of the doorway, poking her head behind her a couple of times before she reached the marble arch leading out into the hallway. She disappeared past thin veils of satiny white fabric draped over poles between the rooms.

Domnica frowned. "Come, now, Kalista. Don't just stand there gawking. Take a seat. Your father will be here soon."

Kalista's eyes narrowed, and she shrugged. There was an indifferent tone to her voice. "He won't do anything."

Domnica hissed. "You coarse-mouthed brat. One day, I hope he does. You'll be seventeen soon, and need to start acting like it."

Kalista pushed thick waves of hair behind her shoulders and lifted her chin.

2

Kalista's Hope

"Not that I expect anything different." Domnica's dark eyes flashed. "But, eventually it'll catch up with you." She got up and took quick steps to Kalista. "And I said to sit down."

Kalista turned to bolt, but not fast enough.

Domnica grabbed her by the shoulder, yanking her back around, and in one swift motion struck Kalista across the cheek hard, causing her to fall backward.

Kalista grabbed the table, catching herself and letting out a painful sound. And then she righted herself. Her face burned, but she wouldn't give her stepmother the satisfaction of acknowledging her actions with words.

Domnica scowled and shoved her down on a bench. She eyed Kalista distastefully. "Serves you right. The least you could have done is to have combed your hair before you came to breakfast. You're of marrying age, Kalista. Camila wouldn't dare leave her room the way you do." She sat back down.

Kalista rubbed her cheek and pursed her lips tighter.

Camila smoothed out her gown. "There's no resemblance, thank the gods."

Both women laughed.

Kalista's eyes burned. She drew her tunic, a green wrap, around her. "It matters little what you have to say to me." She got up from her seat and made her way to the doorway of the room, wanting nothing more than to be done with these two, meddling women. What did she care whether she ate or not?

And then, a curt voice brought her to a halt. "Kalista!"

Immediately, she lowered herself to a curtsy and bowed low. A cold draft swept into the room with her father. Kalista winced. "Father. You didn't hear…"

"Silence." There was an edge to his voice. "There's no need to say anything."

Kalista pursed her lips. She didn't look up, but imagined her father above her, his wide, dark eyes boring into her. There was never a time he didn't seem like a bear on the prowl, ready to devour anyone or anything in his path.

Dominica let out a breath. "Terentius, she's been unruly since she came into the room."

"But…" Kalista interrupted.

"Not another word." Her father's voice lowered.

Kalista looked up and could see a smirk flit across Camila's face. Ignoring it, she lifted her head and went to a long

3

slab of stone. She sat down with her back to the others at the end, half listening to their conversation.

She reached up to quell the stinging in her eyes, a last defense against the tears threatening to spill, and nibbled at full bowls of cheese, fruits and meats set out in front of her, barely noticing the smooth, honey-laden grape drink, as she lifted it to her lips and let it trickle down her throat.

The conversation took a turn, and Kalista bent her head to listen while she sat there without saying anything.

Her father's voice was low. "There are changes. And someone really needs to do something about that religious sect causing all the trouble."

Domnica's eyes narrowed. "The Christians? Again?"

He nodded. "I've been trying to get the council to understand the necessity to come down hard on those people. The potential for an upset in the government's likely. They're meeting secretly and hiding the amount of followers they have."

"Why not the lions? Wouldn't this dissuade their activity?" Domnica's dark eyes suddenly glowed.

Camila feigned shock, yet a smile curved her lips. She popped a grape in her mouth, sucking on the juice.

Terentius frowned. "I think we've more tolerance than that for other religions, regardless of the annoyances they cause."

"But, if they're dangerous. It might just curb their lust for power. I'm sure Nero would agree." Domnica played with the folds of her gown. Her eyes were hard like two marble stones dyed black.

"Probably, but Nero would sell his own mother if given the chance. He's already trying to do away with his wife. There are less sadistic ways to deal with them."

"But if he allows these people freedom, things might not be so good for us in the future."

Terentius sighed. "That might be true. But, we've nothing to accuse them of at this time."

Kalista let out a breath. Christians. Did they have nothing better to do than to try and push their ridiculous religion on others? She took one last drink and put the chalice on the table. "I'm finished. Can I leave, father?"

Terentius waved his hand dismissively at her, not looking up from his plate.

Kalista's Hope

Kalista took her cue and slipped out of the room, edging along the narrow, stone hallway toward the front of the house, waving off servants who tried to follow.

She dutifully stopped by the door to kneel in front of a small corner shrine filled with silver statuettes of the household gods. She lit incense on a stone table, tipping her head toward the tiled floor and mouthed a quick incantation.

She picked up the golden casket god and stared into the hollow space inside. Cold and lifeless, yet she had to give it deference along with hundreds of others that littered the great city of Rome. A chill ran through her as she wondered how she could ever please them all.

She set it back on the shelf, picking up a small statue of Venus, speaking the rote prayer she repeated daily before leaving her home. "Venus, sacred queen, grant me a song of beauty. I call thee with holy, reverent mind." Then she set the statue back on the shelf staring at the other silent metal images on the wall.

She got up, and went to the door, pushing on it and stepping into the inner courtyard, finding her way out the main gate, leaving in the direction of Janus, the ancient god of openings, gateways and doors. Everyday, she prayed he'd help her learn truth.

She clutched a sweet cake she'd taken from the table tightly in her hand and moved in quick strides toward the bustling sounds of the city.

***

"Terentius, you have to do something about your daughter." Domnica's eyes were like slits. "She tries me daily."

He shrugged his shoulders. "Do we have to talk about this?"

"But, she embarrasses the Neo family, and her name's being bandied about the city." She got up from the table, pacing the room.

Terentius sighed. "Use the nanny slave. Tell Nona to be tough with her."

"Nona's afraid of her shadow. Terentius, you're the only one she listens to. *You* must put your foot down. She needs to start improving or we'll be the laughing stock of all our friends. She roams around the town, barely finishing her lessons. She takes no slaves with her. I won't stand for it any longer. You're her father and have control over her and her life…if you know what I mean." She paused for emphasis.

Kara S. McKenzie

Terentius let out an exasperated sound. He stood up. "I've no patience for this. My plans were to fish in the countryside. I'll deal with it another time, and I really don't want to discuss it today. Nona needs to take care of it."

Domnica frowned, but was silent. She watched her husband leave through the open doorway, then turned to her daughter. "Someday…she's going to find herself in more trouble than she knows."

Camila nodded, twisting a strand of silky hair between her fingers. "I saw a girl whipped to death for less trouble than she gives you. I'd never be like that." She turned to the side, revealing a slightly crooked nose, the only outward flaw impossible to hide with the heavy creams and thick make-up. She rose from her seat.

"You're not anything like her." Domnica drew another glass of wine to her lips.

Camila nodded. "And hope I never am."

Her stepmother smiled. "You won't be. And I'm sure you'll improve both our positions. I've great plans for you."

Camila lowered her eyes to her drink. "Yes, mother, I'm sure you do."

***

Kalista raced down a wide path lined with trees leading from the stately Palatine Hill where she lived, onto the street of Argelitum, passing statues, triangular altars and closely quartered stone buildings along the way.

She dodged a chariot, tripping on her tunic and tumbled face first onto the road, masses of tangled auburn hair spilling out around her.

She got up quickly and tried to wipe the dust from her skirt, but was dismayed to find the more she rubbed, the deeper ingrained it became. She let out an annoyed sound, frowning at the thought of what Domnica would say. She picked up the honey cake she dropped on the ground beside her and blew on it.

The temple of Argelitum was in the distance, where Janus was housed, a couple more blocks. She'd offer her honey cake and prayers and then be off to see Justus, her solace after such a morning. He'd been her childhood friend since she was old enough to roam the streets. He always knew how to make her forget her troubles.

She entered the Forum on her way to the temple, past people bartering their farmer's produce and wares. Tall buildings

6

Kalista's Hope

and imposing statues rose to meet the sky on all sides of her. Kalista's eyes were drawn upward. The sky was dismal other than a few small shards of sun attempting to peek through the dark mist that thread its way through the city. But, the tiny bits of light didn't seem to be having much effect.

Despite the morning drizzle, the streets bustled. Vendors hollered their prices, while the clomp of horses feet on cobblestone pounded loudly in Kalista's ears and coarse laughter echoed from the theaters, baths and brothels, spilling out from under arched doorways.

She walked a little further and spotted a small child on the side of the street, wearing a tattered homespun tunic. A slave's child. The young girl got up and came to her, tugging on her gown. "Do you have a sweet cake for me, pretty lady?"

Kalista put her hand to her mouth and held back a laugh. "Pretty lady?" She mimicked the child. "I've not been called that before." Then, she patted the top of the child's head. "Here" She got down on one knee and pulled the young girl close to her. She broke off the good half of the sweet cake and handed it to the girl. "Take this. But, I need to give the rest to Janus." She ruffled the top of the little one's hair.

The young girl reached out and took the cake in her hands and put it in her mouth. She pushed back her mussed hair as she chewed on it. "It's good." Her eyes shone as she looked at Kalista. And then she turned and ran, looking back once.

Kalista got up and dusted off her tunic. She smiled, then got back on the path and started down it.

Further on, she spotted a troop of soldiers, making their way across a thick, stone bridge. Dust billowed around them as they pushed their horses forward, men with shields, carrying swords.

Kalista moved to the side of the road, watching them pass. A thunderous beat drummed within her, as the men stormed over the next bridge and out of sight. They were probably on their way to look for more land and the spoils with it. She wished she could see the places they saw and fight with them. Sometimes, it didn't seem fair that she'd been born a girl.

After the last of them passed, she stopped for a quick moment by the triangular altar next to her. Concordia, the god dedicated to keeping peace in families was inside. The statue's arms were spread in a gesture of harmony.

Kara S. McKenzie

Harmony…in a family? How many times had she offered sweet cakes on this altar and received no reply? She looked away and stepped quickly past. Hiking up her skirt, so as not to trip again, she ran up the path to the gates of Janus.

She went through the massive stone structure. Kneeling, she laid a sweet honey cake at the base of the two-headed god, touching her face to the ground. "Janus, god of beginnings and passageways, I beg you to reveal yourself to me. I petition you with sweet cakes."

She leaned closer to the statue, extending her hand, touching its cold surface, studying the two twin faces, one facing forward, one back. "Speak to me, as you've spoken to the ancients." She tapped the side of the god. "Tell me things of old."

She stopped praying and listened. A chill breeze flittered past her. She tipped her head to the side awaiting a sign, anything but the hushed silence of the day.

She lifted her head again. What was it she really wanted from him? Was she really expecting an answer? Would one sign be impossible for the oldest of Roman gods?

She thought if she got to Janus early enough, before the morning crowd, he might be willing to offer her something. But, he didn't. Why should this day be different?

She prayed this prayer more than once for Janus to reveal himself to her, but his twin chiseled faces surely had no time for the likes of her.

A bird flew up and lit on Mar's helmet and then dropped down behind the statue onto the ground, pecking crumbs of honey cake. At least the birds would enjoy a meal her sweet cakes would offer.

She heard a sound outside the gates and tiptoed to the entrance. Footsteps?

She peered around the opening.

A man, who looked to be a few years older than her, wrapped in a toga of the plebian class, reached into a bag he carried and pulled out a couple pieces of folded parchment. His sun-lightened hair reached just over his ears, and his profile revealed a well-formed nose with a prominent bridge, typical of many Roman men. He wasn't poor, judging from his clothing, and yet not of her class, either.

Kalista's breath caught slightly in her throat, as her eyes swept over his solid frame and handsome profile. She was sure he wasn't one to go unnoticed in the social circles.

8

Kalista's Hope

A young servant ran to the man, taking the parchment from his hands and smiled. They exchanged quick greetings and spent a brief moment in conversation.

Kalista took a step forward, curious, then stayed where she was, until each of them nodded and headed off in different directions.

As the boy turned toward town, Kalista noticed one of the small scrolls the man had given him slipped from his hand to the ground. She remained in place, wondering if he'd come back for it.

When she realized she was alone, she crept around the corner and picked up the parchment and began to read. She frowned at the small symbol of a fish at the top. Christians, and Romans at that.

She let out a breath. And she had even contemplated introducing herself to them. What a waste that such an attractive looking man should turn out to be one of them?

She read quickly. *Meeting – two days after Sabbath, dusk– change location – house of Narcissus.*

Hmm? She contemplated bringing the note home to show her father, but realized she might get more information if she spied on them instead.

She smiled to herself, and then laid the note back on the ground. Whether the boy returned or not to retrieve it, she was quite certain the meeting would still take place. And she was sure it would be at the home of the Narcissus she knew, being it was on this side of town.

"Kalista!"

She swung round when she recognized a voice behind her.

"Justus! I was on my way to your place."

A tall, rather thin, young man lifted an arm and pointed at the gates. "I was at the forum and knew you'd probably stop at Janus first. I thought I might walk back with you."

She smiled. "I'd like that."

He held up the edge of her tunic as if to inspect it. "How did you manage this?

Kalista's brows knit together. She brushed a strand of hair from her eyes and wiped the edge of her dusty tunic. "It's only a little dust."

He smiled. "I suppose you want to go to my father's home."

"Anything would be better than my place."

9

Justus nodded. "But, don't you have schooling with Nona?"

She made a face. "You know they don't care where I am. Father's hunting, and I suspect Domnica and Camila will be busy in the Forum today. I'll be back late, and by then, they'll be too tired to take any action."

He nodded again. "Well, father has books you might like."

She tipped her head and let out a sigh of relief. "Good. That's the best thing I've heard today. I can't wait to see them. Let's get out of here."

Justus smiled. "At least you like our books."

She laughed, taking his arm. "Why I keep you as a friend."

He laughed with her, walking by her side.

Their steps grew longer and faster as they headed down the road in the general direction of Justus' apartment.

***

Chapter 2

The cramped, mud-brick home provided little space for movement in the clutter of dusty books stacked in rows on shelves about the room. Other furniture was scarce. A wooden table was crammed against a corner furthest from the door with two stools next to it. On an opposite wall, two sleeping mats hung from an iron hook.

"Father, it's Kalista. She's come to look at the books."

Rufinus Ovidius, a stoop-back, mousy-haired man moved about the room with an awkward gait, poking at his possessions, occasionally repositioning a book or rechecking his list of supplies to sell on the streets. He eyed Kalista nervously, wringing his hands. "Be careful. You know I like them handled properly."

"She knows this."

Kalista nodded.

Rufinus sat down on a stool, while Kalista and Justus read titles.

Kalista gently lifted a book off the stack and blew dust off the parchment. She smiled at the fact Justus' father didn't want any re-positioning of the books, but didn't seem concerned with the thick particles settled on them. "Look at this." She ran her fingers over the title.

"Poetry?"

"Lucretius Carus."

"Hmm. Not one I'd think you'd read." Justus leaned closer.

"It's about the natural man and the foolishness of religion, simple superstitions others are led to believe in."

"Oh? Well, maybe I'm wrong." He eyed it with a new interest. And then he began to cough.

Kalista noticed the short intake of his breath. The dust was bothering him again.

His father called out to him. "Get some air, son."

"Go." Kalista waved him to the balcony. "I'm almost finished."

Justus got up and waded through the stacks of books, making his way across the room. He opened the door and stepped out, closing it behind him.

Kalista fingered the stack of literature on the floor beside her, her hands resting on a thicker book near the top of the stack. What interested her more than the book itself was a piece of folded parchment sticking out from inside the front cover. It was a letter, but she couldn't quite make out what it said. She was surprised Justus' father hadn't noticed it before and wondered who might have put it there and why.

Justus' father was so engrossed in his paperwork, thumbing through stacks of work on the table, she knew if she were to shift the parchment from one book to the other, he'd never notice. Her temptation was greater than her sense of honor, so she barely thought twice about what she was doing, and within seconds managed to slip the mysterious piece of paper from the book in the stack, to the one she held tightly in her hand.

She gingerly ran her fingers through a strand of hair that fell over her shoulder and bit her lower lip. After paying for the book, she tiptoed cautiously, making her way out onto the balcony and stood beside Justus.

She looked out over the city and put her hand to her chest. The view never failed to take her breath away.

Justus' apartment was eight stories above the ground overlooking Rome, which extended as far as the eye could see, between the hills surrounding it. Kalista was awed by the powerful magnificence of the city with its solid stone gates on the outer wall, and the many buildings set out in neat rows beneath them. Massive statues sat on every corner of the street.

"Did you find a good one?" Justus lifted his hand to his mouth, as if to hold back another cough.

"I paid your father for the one I showed you."

"I wondered if you'd get it." He looked pleased.

He gestured to a chair. "So stay? And we'll read together for a while."

"I'd love to. Anything to keep me from Palantine Hill."

Kalista sank comfortably into one of the curved backed chairs and spent the day with Justus reading and soaking in the sun that occasionally peeked out from beneath the passing clouds. She relished in the time she spent in his home and dreaded going back to her own.

Time quickly passed, as the shadows of the day lengthened. And when she noticed dusk closing in upon them, she got up and closed her book. "I didn't realize it was getting this late. It looks like I have to go."

Kalista's Hope

He nodded. "I'll take you back." And then he coughed again.

Kalista frowned. "No. You stay. You shouldn't be out. You've done enough today."

"But, you know the streets. It's night, and they're not safe."

"Don't worry. I'll be fine."

He held up a hand, but only a wheeze came out.

"See." She wagged a finger at him. "How many times have I've made this trip on my own. It'll be no different tonight."

Justus took her arm. His voice was raspy. "But, things haven't been good lately, especially in the evening hours. And you've changed. You're not a young girl anymore. And..." He looked a little embarrassed to say more.

Kalista frowned. "Believe me. There's no cause for concern. There are others who should worry more than I should."

Justus shook his head. "At least try to be careful. I'll pray the gods will be with you."

She nodded. "Thank you. This I can use."

And with that she left, finding her way down the stairs and onto the streets, turning, and waving only once from the steps below.

The sun was setting and darkness was creeping in. Few people were out, and Kalista realized it was later than she thought. Storm clouds lay on the horizon. She quickened her steps on the street, drawing her cloak tighter about her, feeling less brave than she'd admit, hugging to the shadows of the walls.

Two drunken militia stumbled by, uttering profanities, and she stopped briefly to let them pass. Neither seemed interested in a disheveled young woman with wild red sprigs of hair poking out from beneath her bedraggled cloak.

She thought about what her stepmother and Camila had said to her that morning. She worried that her days of roaming through the city were coming an end soon. She was getting too old for the type of life she led, and her father wouldn't put up with it for long. Her situation had been an advantage to her in some ways, having been allowed more freedom than girls naturally had. But, even this couldn't go on forever.

As she turned the next corner, she heard a commotion. She squinted in the dark, but couldn't see anything. There were muffled sounds of laughter and a loud knock on a door.

13

She edged closer to the wall and waited, silent. The streets cast an eerie glow in the distance, yet the low hanging fog blurred her vision, and she couldn't make out the shadowy figures drawing closer.

There was a sound behind her. She whirled around. But, before she could react, she was dragged into an alley. Unable to right herself against the rough stone beneath her feet, she fought to yank herself from the stranger's hold. A hand fixed over her mouth. Why hadn't she been more careful? What trap had she let herself fall into?

"Quiet." A man's voice cautioned her.

She attempted to squeeze out of his grasp, but when she realized it was impossible, she took a hard swing and connected with the side of his face.

"Ow!" He let out a sound and loosened his grip.

Kalista took her chance and hastily broke free from him and began running down the alley. But, before she could get to the street, she tripped, falling on the stone path, unable to right herself before the man's arms came around her a second time, and his hand clamped over her mouth. This time she couldn't break free from his strong hold.

"It's Nero, you fool!" He whispered in her ear. "Do you want him to hear you?"

Before she could answer, a scream rang out across the street. A young woman cried out. "Nooo! Let me stay! Please, I don't want to go with you! Father!"

The fog lifted briefly, and Kalista made out the light of two torches held by shadowed men standing above a huddled figure on the ground. The men staggered and laughed, poking at a young woman who was wracked with sobs, balancing shakily on her knees in the middle of the street. Another, presumably her father, was lying prostrate next to her, pleading. "Please!"

Kalista shivered, noticing the crown on one of the men's heads. Nero, was on the streets?

He stood in the middle of the group.

Kalista pried the man's fingers from her mouth and stared at the scene playing out in front of her, her lips parting slightly. She whispered to herself, "By the gods."

The man who held the power of Rome beneath his fingertips, the emperor, was standing a few cubits from her. She gazed at him in rapt silence.

Kalista's Hope

He was shorter in stature then she remembered. He hovered over the girl on the street in the torchlight. He was wrapped in a sort of dressing gown of purple, and was wearing no belt or shoes. A glittering crown of jewels shifted precariously on the top of his stringy hair. A gold scarf fell about his neck in disarray. He laughed a drunken sound, losing his balance. His gown slid carelessly over his shoulder.

The young woman's father rose slightly. "Please, your grace!" The pain in his voice was evident. "I've no other children."

Kalista wanted to go out in the street and beg for the man, so desperate were his cries, but knew she could do nothing for the girl and would be putting herself in the same jeopardy. It pained her to know there was none who could stand up to the emperor and that he could destroy her, or anyone else he wanted to, in a word. She watched him, her eyes narrowing to slits. No one person should have such power.

Nero convulsed with laughter. He lowered his voice, as he leaned nearer the father. "If you breathe another word, you'll not see her again, and she'll not live beyond this night." He touched the young woman's hair. "But, she'll be back to you, soon enough. When I decide." A leering grin spread over his features.

The father looked pained, yet was silent.

Kalista shuddered at the young woman's fate. She'd heard tales of Nero's lecherous deeds at his palace. Her heart ached for the father lying on the street, helpless to save his own daughter. She imagined the pain he felt.

Nero motioned to his friends. "Take her!"

One of the men bent over and seized the girl by the hair, yanking her from the ground, ignoring her screams. He shoved her ahead of him, smirking as she reluctantly took steps down the street. She wept as she stumbled alongside three other young women. She looked back at her father, taking one last glance as she was torn from him.

The emperor's minstrels played music, while the group disappeared from view. The father was left behind wailing on the street, where he was comforted by others and carried into the safety of his home.

Kalista covered her mouth with her hands. She held back a sob and wiped away a tear.

She felt a hand on her arm, tugging at her to stand.

15

Kara S. McKenzie

"Nero might've seen you if I hadn't done something."
The man's voice behind Kalista was brusque but quiet, too.

Immediately she yanked her arm free. She got up and
gripped the wall behind her, swinging around. "You might have
warned me as to what you were doing?" She peered into the
shadows, but couldn't see his face.

"And risk Nero? You saw what happened to the girl."

"He might've seen us anyway, with all the noise you
made."

The man let out a breath. "It's true. I suppose I
underestimated you."

Kalista's fists clenched. Her face was hard like stone.
"How can men do such things?" She wondered aloud, wishing
she could lash out at someone for it.

"They say he's mad. And only one man."

Kalista turned. "Hmph. I've seen others, no better than
him."

The clouds drifted past the moon allowing for more light.
Kalista had to catch her breath when she saw his face. "You?"
she sputtered accusatory, realizing he was the same man at the
wall outside the Gates of Janus, she'd seen earlier.

She took a step back, unnerved suddenly, by his close
proximity. His eyes were intent on her, as he pushed his tousled
hair back from his face. There was something deep and all
consuming in his expression, and she suddenly felt hesitant and
uneasy next to him.

**

Gaius frowned. Had he seen this waif of a young woman
before? He hadn't thought so. And yet, she seemed to recognize
him?

She was slight in form and delicate featured, with large,
luminous eyes. Her hair, as disheveled as it was, was the loveliest
bright shade of auburn he'd ever seen, and soft looking to the
touch.

He was shocked at the dust on her clothing and face, and
wanted to reach out and brush it from her cheek, uncovering the
pale, silken-looking skin beneath. Her tunic was torn, and she had
a wild look to her, akin to a beaten down slave or an orphan on
the street. And yet, something told him, she wasn't either. She
was an enigma to him.

He felt a stab of sympathy for the young woman, seeing
the distrustful look in her eyes, and what he imagined to be

16

Kalista's Hope

hidden pain that seemed to be emanating from deep within her. She was both beautiful in looks, as she seemed pitiful in spirit.

***

Kalista remembered what she planned to do, and couldn't let this man's kind expression, sway her sound judgment. "Oh...I mean...it's only you resembled someone I saw on the streets today." She was wary under his watchful eye. She knew her tunic was shambled, and her face was dirty. She pushed her untamed hair behind her, wishing for once she would have combed it, wanting nothing to do with piteous glances from this man.

He eyed her curiously, as he stood there on the street.

She frowned, wondering at his thoughts. "Why do you stare like you do?"

Gaius smiled. "I think I might've noticed *you*, if we'd met before."

She didn't like the way he said it. Her eyes narrowed, and she took a step back. "I'm sure you would've noticed me, but it wouldn't have mattered what you thought."

He suddenly reached out, touching the sleeve of her tunic. "It's not of the lower class. You're not from this part of town, are you?"

She moved her arm out of his grasp. "My home isn't anywhere near here." Her brow furrowed.

"Then I've misjudged you again."

He looked down and suddenly eyed her bare feet peeking out from under her gown. He began to smile. An amused look crossed his face.

Her cheeks rose in flame, and her lips drew into a line. "And so you have misjudged me. Yet, your opinion matters little to me." She took hold of the wall and stepped out of the alley, keeping her distance, trying to appear composed, but feeling as if she were failing miserably.

He studied her again, as he took a place alongside her. "So, where *do* you live?"

Kalista moved quickly on the cobblestone street, not looking up.

He nudged her shoulder with his own. "You don't have to say. But, it's late, and I intend to walk with you, so I *will* know soon enough."

17

Kalista let out a breath and lifted her chin. "You may not want to walk with me, when you know how far I have to go. It's not a small distance, on one of the hills."

"The hills? In your bare feet?"

Kalista frowned at him, then diverted her eyes again from his curious gaze. The man truly disconcerted her. "It won't bother me. I'm used to it. Now, will you please let me alone? I want to be home before morning." She tugged on her disheveled gown to keep from stumbling and took quick steps to his long, unhurried ones, all the while trying to keep her eyes from his scrutinizing stare.

His mouth lifted at the corners. "But, I don't know your name?"

Her brow slanted downward, and she didn't answer.

"You don't have to tell me, but I did keep you from Nero. You might oblige me for this. And you shouldn't be afraid to tell me."

She fumed silently inside. Afraid? Of him? Not hardly?

She lifted her hand to her eyes to block out the glow of the rising moon so she could look at him. She let out a breath. "You hardly kept me from him. But, my name's Kalista, if you feel you must know."

She didn't turn away. She met his gaze with a bold stare. She wasn't afraid of anyone.

He didn't say anything at first.

She could see that he was older than she'd guessed, possibly in his early thirties. And even taller than she'd imagined, her chin barely reaching his chest.

He smiled, studying her with interest. "Hmm. I thought your name might be Pompieana or something like that, after the volcano, with that hair and temper. I'm sure I'll have a black eye by morning." He laughed, good-naturedly. "But, I think I like Kallie. It goes better with your personality."

She turned in the light of the moon, a flame heating her cheeks. "I don't care what you call me. But, I assure you. I didn't give you a black eye and didn't hit you that hard."

He laughed again. "I suppose I'll know tomorrow. For such a slight girl, you have a solid right arm."

Kalista didn't reply, turning her eyes back to the road. She shivered at the thought of walking alone, but wasn't sure she wanted the company of this man and his light ribbing along the way, either.

18

Kalista's Hope

He chuckled, as if amused by her silence. He pointed to his eye. "I suppose I shouldn't say more or I'm likely to get into trouble with you again."

She couldn't help her lip curling upward at the thought of his remark.

They walked a distance in silence until they came to the Arch of Augustus.

They passed two Roman guards and stepped under the stone gateway and into the forum. Music and laughter spilled out onto the streets from the taverns, and a dog yelped in the distance. Other than these sounds, the streets were quiet in the wake of the earlier vendor traffic.

"So, which hill do you live on?" The young man looked curious, eying her tunic again.

Her face was guarded. She really didn't want to reveal a whole lot about herself. Her voice stuck in her throat, but she cleared it. "Palatine."

He let out a whistle. "Palatine! Who's your father?"

She stiffened. There was a brief silence, before she answered again. Her tone was curt. "You'll know soon enough."

He shrugged his shoulders, not saying anything, but regarded her with an interested look.

Kalista followed the moonlit path over the cobblestone suddenly uncomfortable with the man's unceasing glances her way. The coolness of the night should've been refreshing, but a heavy feeling began to weigh on her, and a sense of dread crept into her chest. For reasons she didn't understand, it bothered her when any stranger tried to ask too many questions of her. Even Justus knew she was a closed book when it came to revealing too much of herself.

She tried to shake the anxious feeling inside her off, but couldn't. Great, she thought. Not here. This is the last thing she wished to happen, in front of this man.

Lately, these attacks had been plaguing her more often. She'd only recently visited the doctor concerning her plight, but was told there was nothing anyone could do for her, and that it was a condition brought on by the anxiety within her. She wished she knew how to stop it. On this night, she'd no desire for this man to see her lack of control over it.

But, she couldn't consider any of that now when her chest was beginning to feel as if it were caving in, and her breathing was getting heavier by the moment. Her breath started to come in

19

short catches, and she stopped walking. She leaned forward, pressing her hand on her chest.

"Kallie? Are you all right?" The young man edged up to her.

She clutched herself again and tried to draw in air, but could manage only in tiny gulps. She held up her hand, turning away from him.

"What's wrong?" He reached out and took hold of her arm.

Tears began to fill her eyes, and she sat down on the ground, drawing her knees up to her chest. She turned away from him, not wanting to talk and not able to. She pushed her hair behind her and rocked back and forth.

He squatted beside her and put his hand on her shoulder, speaking quietly. "Please. Breathe slowly, and try to be calm. Take it easy."

And then he held her wrist firmly. "Here," he spoke almost inaudibly. "You'll be all right." He didn't release his hold, quietly talking to her all the while.

Kallie leaned closer, tense at first and then began to rest easier. She'd never known what it felt like to be treated so tenderly by anyone, as it was never offered to her, even as a small child. She was spellbound by his kindness and care.

She took longer, more concentrated puffs of air, and then waited for her breaths to slow, unclenching her fists and feeling the tension in her lesson.

He set her aside, stroking her hair and whispering quietly to her. "There. You'll be all right, now. Just slow your breaths."

She looked up, meeting his clear, steady blue eyes. The kindness in them confused her.

She wiped the tears from her face.

He took her hand, holding it firmly. "Is it better?"

Her mouth parted, and she nodded. Her breathing was constant again. "Yes. It's all right, now."

He got up and pulled her up beside him. "Are you sure?" He looked as if he were truly concerned.

There was something different about this man, and she wasn't sure how she felt about it. She began to turn away, nodding. "Yes."

He didn't let go of her, still holding her hand firmly in his grasp, reaching up to push a thick strand of her hair back from her face.

Kalista's Hope

Her eyes narrowed suspiciously, and she pried her fingers from his. She moved away, trying to distance herself from him. "I said I'm all right. You can let go."

His face was full of questions. "I'm sorry. I only wanted to make sure you were not having anymore difficulty." He began up the path again and moved next to her, as she strode ahead. "Has this happened before?"

She eyed him warily. "Yes. But, really, it's nothing. The doctor said he couldn't do anything about it."

"So, it happens often?" He looked concerned.

Kalista frowned, not wanting to discuss, what she felt was a weakness in her. "Please. It doesn't matter. It's over now."

He didn't question further, but walked next to her on the path up the hillside in silence.

Kalista wondered what he would think when he found out who she was and where she lived. Would his behavior change toward her? Would he suddenly wish for more from her, or to ask her for a favor, as so many others had before him?

She begrudgingly took steps up the path that led to her palace home and took him to the gate.

His eyes widened when she stopped in front of it. "You're Terentius Neo's daughter?"

She gave him an indifferent look, answering him curtly. "And you're impressed?"

At first he began to smile and then looked as if he thought better of it. He shrugged. "Just surprised. I wouldn't have thought his daughter would be out so late at night alone."

Kalista ignored his comment. He needn't know everything about her. She unlatched the gated entrance and slipped into the courtyard passing two large statues of lions on both sides of the path. "No one's here. Come. You can go with me to the door."

He went in through the gate behind her. They stopped in front of the entrance to the home. "No one to greet you?" He was puzzled.

Her eyes darkened. "They aren't waiting up. You must trust what I say."

She opened the door to go inside, then stopped and looked back. "I hope you haven't regretted coming as far as you did. I could've come by myself and would've been all right."

He gave her a serious look. "Kallie. You might not have been all right. And with the difficulties you had with breathing,

21

Kara S. McKenzie

you should have someone with you. You really shouldn't be out alone at night. It isn't safe." He shook his head. "I hope you won't do this again, or at least take a trustworthy friend with you."

She looked back at him reluctantly and nodded. "I can't promise anyone anything, but I thank you for walking with me." Her cheeks reddened at the thought of allowing a total stranger to have taken such care for her like he did. She could barely look at him. "And for helping."

She closed the door, not waiting for his answer. She went to one of the windows, watching him leave the through the gate, realizing she never did learn the man's name.

She made her way up the stairs and walked to her room, hoping she could slip quietly inside.

***

"Kalista! Camila glowered. "Nona! Come quick and get her into a bath! She smells."

Kalista frowned, as she came through the doorway, upon hearing the slave bustling down the hallway toward their bedroom.

Nona poked her head in the door nervously and wrung her hands. "Come with me, miss. I'll take you to the bath and get you cleaned up."

***

Chapter 3

The family gathered at the household altar for their daily ritual, along with Nona and a few of the other slaves who lined the opposite wall.

Kalista shivered from the cold drafty walls of the room and edged herself closer to a small streak of sunlight making it's way in through an opening in the center of the room. She was glad she chose to strap on her sandals, as she knew the mosaic tiles beneath her bare feet would feel like winter on a day such as this.

Her father stooped to light incense, offering prayers to their family Lares, then chanted to the gods. When he finished, Domnica and Camila both knelt, picking up silver statuettes and kissing them, offering their own muffled incantations.

Kalista rolled her eyes, silently speculating how these two women could appease a god with their malicious hearts. Yet, some gods could be as spiteful and full of vengeance as the two of them, so maybe their antics would be overlooked.

The more books she read about the gods, the more confused she was. With her religion's mixture of fragmented rituals, superstitions, and taboos collected over years from other societies and civilizations, there seemed little in it to trust. She wished her own mother were here to help her understand.

Kalista recalled the last visit she made to her mother's tomb, during the Festival of Parentalia. She'd poured perfume over the urn in efforts to appease the spirits, a duty her father neglected. She wanted no part in welcoming the ghosts of the grave of her ancestors into her city or home by leaving the tomb in shambles.

The inscription on the stone roiled emotions within her, and she shoved tears away remembering it. Her father must have loved her mother very much to have written such beautiful prose and include it on the tomb. She yearned to have known him before her mother's death.

She memorized what he'd had etched into the stone marker.

> *'To release my darling wife, Gabriella, to the earth this day,*
> *was toughest price for anyone to pay.*

Kara S. McKenzie

No more her jeweled eyes to light my path,
or her delightful smile to gentle my untamed wrath...'

Delightful smile, jeweled eyes, darling. Kalista sighed. If she could only have witnessed her father so happy. Things surely would've been different if her mother had lived. The first words on the stone spoke volumes to Kalista, and she hung onto each and every one of them.

She watched her father who was still praying and wondered why he seemed to care so little for her, when his feelings for her natural mother were so obvious. He looked up briefly, and his dark eyes turned to stone when they met hers.

Immediately, the rest of the epitaph came to her mind, and her heart felt as if a knife had stabbed her chest as she thought of it.

'A stolen sweet replaced that solemn night,
By flaming, crying babe to dim the light.
And I may ask that earth you take my darling's pain,
and bestow on her the peace I'll never know again.'

She winced. Stolen sweet, her mother. Stolen away, never to steal her father's heart, again.

And flaming babe? She twirled a strand of fiery hair around her finger and tossed it behind her. She was doomed to bear the guilt her father pinned on her since she was born.

She stood up straighter, her eyes frosting over. What did it matter whether he cared or not?

After the rituals were finished, Kalista disappeared from the room. She was loath to speak to Camila or have words with her stepmother. Both reminded her of what she didn't have, and she had no desire to linger in this place with either of them. As far as she was concerned, they were no better than those black-hearted serpents that writhed on the top of Medusa's head. And just has horrid looking, too.

***

Across the city, a woman of an equally destructive force, stirred in the palace.

"Get up, Nero. It's almost noon. And get that conniving woman out of your room. Where's your wife?" Agrippina thrust back thick, red curtains allowing a crack of light into the shadowy room. She looked like a raven-haired lioness, ready to pounce upon the girl lying next to her son. Dark kohl lining her blue eyes emphasized the intensity in them. The gold leaf crown upon her

Kalista's Hope

head held black ringlets, threatening to spill from behind her shoulders.

Poppaea glowered, her green eyes flashing. She rose up, drawing the golden wrap on the chair around her. "Nero, it's early." Her red lips twisted into a pout. "My love, must it always come to this?"

Nero dismissively waved the young woman away with his hand. She quickly got up, but swiveled around to toss him a seductive smile. She paraded past Agrippina with a triumphant air, the thin, filmy clothing she wore exemplifying her shapely figure beneath.

When the door slammed shut, Agrippina's eyes lit, as if on fire. She looked angry enough to reach out and choke her son. "Well? Where's your wife?" She moved closer to Nero, hard lines in her face deepening.

"Octavia's gone, mother." He propped himself to a sitting position, wrapping a green dressing gown around him lazily. He looked bored.

"Gone?" Agrippina's eyes sparked. "What do you mean *gone*." Her voice sounded as if it suddenly had raised three octaves.

Nero snorted in laughter. "I've learned from you, mother. Maybe, someday I'll just toss her out. Poppaea's much more interesting, if you understand what I mean." He gave her a sidelong glance, a smile worming its way across his face, seeming almost pleased by her distress.

Agrippina bristled, looking at him as if he'd lost his mind. "Octavia's your wife, Nero. Remember that." She drew her outer wrap tighter around her, gripping it in her fist.

He looked annoyed. "Octavia was a sacrificial lamb, and you know it. She was all your doing." He lifted a glass of wine resting on a stand next to his bed, then pressed his hand to his head and took a drink.

Agrippina's cat-like eyes narrowed. "I raised you better than this."

"Better? Poisoning father and my stepbrother? So I could have the throne?" Nero's face reddened. There was something ominous in his expression. "I feel sorry for you, mother. What do you expect with your own ill-fated marriage?"

His mother's eyes turned dark as a pit. "You were young and don't understand what your father put me through. You don't remember how I tried so diligently to do the honorable thing."

Kara S. McKenzie

"Honorable?" Nero sneered. He took another swig of wine, wiping his mouth with the back of his hand. "I knew him better than you thought I did."

Even though Agrippina fumed with rage, she said nothing. Better not to follow that path. She knew how utterly undone he could become if she tried to defend her position against his father. It was difficult to compete with a dead man, even if his demise was his own doing.

Nero frowned. "Please, mother. Out with it. I'm not fooled by your silence. I know that mute fury of yours."

But, when she still didn't answer, he looked thoroughly annoyed and let out a wounded sound. "You believed you could control me because I was young. But, you can't do that anymore. I'm emperor, now."

Agrippina's voice lowered to a purr. "But you don't remember everything, Nero. Your father wasn't a model citizen. I had reasons to take the measures I did."

His face contorted slightly. "Oh, mother...I was old enough to know more than you think. And I...*knew* about the mushrooms."

Agrippina gasped. "None of it was truth, Nero. You couldn't know."

"But you brought them to him. I saw." Nero smiled, a half-deranged look on his face.

She colored slightly, a red streak spreading up her neck. "But, I keep telling you there was more to it than you know. Your father..."

"My father!" Nero slammed his fist into the table next to him. "I don't want you to talk about him anymore, not when he's not here to defend himself!"

Agrippina flinched. "But, how can I *explain?*"

"Mother. You might have pulled my puppet strings, when I was younger, but I'm twenty-three. It's not necessary for you to *explain* anything." He shivered as the chill of the morning air came through the window. The rays of the sun were stronger by the minute, and he reached up as if the pain in his head had intensified.

He looked out, suddenly wistful. "Oh, that it were night again. I enjoyed it so much more than this."

Agrippina moved closer, the anger in her face replaced with a hurt expression. "You might not like me stopping by and ruining your fun, but you need to remember Nero honey, what

26

Kalista's Hope

I've done for you. Don't you remember who fixed you on the throne and got you the coveted position you have now?" She fingered the silken fabric covering him, her eyes taking a form of rapt adoration.

Nero's eyes rolled back, and he sighed an exasperated sound. "I'm not a child, anymore. I've held this position for some time, so please...stop. You must know how tired I am of your drama. I don't need it. I've seen enough of it at the theater."

Agrippina smoothed back a tuft of his hair that had dropped forward. "I only want to help, dearest. Please. Only spend a little time with Octavia, my love. And if you do, you might be able to work this out."

"Mother...are you listening?" Nero nearly howled at her. "I don't want to spend time with Octavia. I never did. She's one of your puppets and a favorite of all your aristocratic friends I despise. I've a mind to divorce her."

Agrippina choked out a sound, as if horrified. "Nero. Think. The people adore Octavia, and you're distancing yourself from the ones who matter."

Nero frowned. "I don't care about *the ones who matter*! I'm dog-tired of playing the puppet for you. I'm done with it!"

The room became gravely silent, and Nero waved his hand at his mother. "Enough! Go away! My head aches, and I don't want to speak of it anymore!"

Agrippina dipped her head in a disparaging manner. "I'm sorry, Nero. I only wished to help. My hope is that someday you might see *my* side of things."

Nero let out a breath, as he watched her make her way slowly out of the room.

Only when the door closed soundly behind her, did he feel his tranquility returning. The woman drove him thoroughly mad at times, unable to admit to the past misdeeds she'd participated in. And in addition to this this, were her daily confrontations and obstructions to his plans. He felt haggard whenever he spent time in her company, and wished for the day to be rid of her.

He realized as of late, it just might be beneficial for him to move her to another residence.

He downed the last of the wine in his cup. One, far from the palace.

A self-satisfied grin stole over his face as he set the cup on a tray next to him. Poppaea suggested the riverside estate in Misenum. He was beginning to believe it might just be the

Kara S. McKenzie

perfect place. Yes, Misenum. First the move, then if this didn't help, further measures might be necessary to be carried out.

***

Kalista curled up in a lounge chair in her bedroom, the small space she loved more than any other room in the home. Her eyes were drawn to the colorful frescos in reds and yellows painted on the walls on all sides. Columns housing the beautiful golden god, Diana Lucina, filled the spaces of one whole wall. Other frescos displayed mountains and bridges with blue birds singing and country villas in picturesque scenes. The small room was decorated sparsely, yet the frescos brought it to life.

She took out the writings of Lucretius Carus and began to read, taking her mind from her troubled thoughts.

As she scanned the words, pieces of parchment dropped onto the floor. She realized it was the letter she'd slipped into the pages of the book at Justus' home. She picked it up and turned it over in her hands.

She skimmed the title, the writings of Paul the Roman? She'd heard of him, a man in the Christian sect causing all kinds of trouble. Curious, her eyes were drawn to the message. She realized it might be something she could report to her father.

As she began to scan the information, she was drawn deeper into it, trying to make sense of the frustrating passages. She didn't quite understand how some of the Roman people actually believed such things, especially those who had no Hebrew ancestry.

The letter went on to explain the workings of this Hebrew God, who Kalista had never heard of.

The second message in the book demonstrated how these people were to live, which was even more surprising to Kalista. It spoke of unity, humility and love and also emphasized the need for a life of charity, forbearance and submission.

How odd? Her eyes drew into a frown. What about war? How could they have respect for themselves without it?

She let out a snort. These people sounded like a bunch of weak, spineless creatures.

She folded the pages and put them back in her book of poems.

Then, she remembered the man who helped her in the alley. Not exactly the feeble sort. On the contrary, he'd risked his own life helping her, in spite of Nero and his men.

28

Kalista's Hope

Likewise, Paul didn't seem like a man without courage, and was a Christian. It didn't make sense. But, neither did her religion.

If only her mother were still alive and might be able to shed light on so many things she didn't understand.

At least Kalista wouldn't treat her mother like Nero did his. She recently heard how he so much as cast the woman out of his life. He'd sent her to a place far from the castle to live, his birth mother, of all people. All because of Poppaea, that ridiculously conniving woman, he couldn't say no to, wanted her out.

Kalista couldn't comprehend it. She'd give anything to have known her mother. Who could be so foolish?

Yet, from what she heard, Nero's birth mother was probably not a whole lot different from Domnica. And if this were the case, she couldn't quite blame him for wanting to be away from her. If Domnica was her natural mother, and she held the power of the throne, Kalista surmised she would've done away with the woman a long time ago.

She took a small, wooden box out of a drawer in her bed stand. As she opened it, her eyes welled up with tears. A pair of earrings, each supporting a small, jade stone with a dangling pearl lay inside, and her fingers brushed them lightly. She wiped a tear away and swore under her breath that someday she'd go to Pompeii and learn more about the other side of her family.

Embedded in her heart from the time she was little were thoughts of the day she'd escape her father and stepmother, and find her way there. She couldn't wait to see the place where her mother's family came from.

She looked back down at the jewels in her hand, suddenly running her fingers lovingly over the jade earrings, holding them close to her.

She smiled. There was no need to regard her viperish stepmother, anymore. It wouldn't be long now, and things would be different. Soon enough, she'd be able to leave Rome and make a new life for herself, and Domnica would be out of hers for good. For years, she stashed money away for this purpose, and she only had to find a way for this dream to come true. Her birth mother's land, held the promise of a different life, one where she might start fresh.

Kalista closed the box and slipped it back into the drawer, thanking Nona under her breath, for preserving her mother's pearls and giving them to her. It was one tie that bound her to her past. And someday, she'd see that past come back to life.

***

Chapter 4

Kalista adjusted her wrinkled tunic as she sat in the stands of the Circus Maximus. She didn't usually care what she wore, but today chose a blue gown to match the flag she carried.

She looked out over the massive, oval-shaped stadium, the largest structure in the city. It took her breath away, just being there. Someone said the place could hold up to two hundred and fifty thousand people at a time, and by the looks of the crowd, she didn't doubt it.

She spun in her seat, the knot of her fiery, sun-scorched hair on the back of her head falling loose from its hold. She shoved the disheveled strands behind her. She was pleased to have convinced Justice so easily to come with her to the track to watch the races. Anything was better than being in that house with Domnica and her stepsister.

With the crowds as loud as they were, she was surprised she could still hear the men below, shouting to the people, as they moved the horses into position to begin the race.

Kalista was halfway from top of the stands. From where she sat, the stadium looked almost as if it were alive, as people streamed through the many doorways by the hundreds in their brightly colored togas and colorful outer wraps.

She wondered if the man she'd met the night before was in the stands, too. More than likely he was, with more than a quarter of Rome watching the races. But, it was near impossible to spot him anywhere in a crowd as this.

The riders on the track bowed and moved into position, ready to start. Kalista put her hand on her chest and took a quick breath. What would it be like to ride like a man, with the speed and agility she could only dream of? She eyed the racers with a wistful expression. "I wish girls could race."

Justus laughed. "And you'd be the first in line with your chariot?" He pushed his elbow into her ribs, poking fun at her.

She frowned, shoving him back. And then a spark lit her eye. "And you know it, too. I would. And, it's not fair that I can't."

He laughed again. "You should've been born a boy. I think you'd have liked it better that way, even though you don't look like one." He tugged on her tunic.

Kara S. McKenzie

Kalista rolled her eyes at him, ignoring the comment. She strained in her seat, waiting for the race to begin.

She liked the fact that events such as this took her mind from the things at home she wanted to forget. Domnica's rages against her had gotten worse the last few weeks, and Camila seemed to be trying to pick a fight with her whenever they were in the room together. She was tired of her stepsister's snide comments, and the fact that no one seemed to notice how cruel she could be. Her father turned a deaf ear, and he too, never failed to show his disapproval of her whenever the opportunity presented itself.

Here at the track, she could leave all of it behind and put her mind to other things, instead.

Her eyes were fixed on the starting line. The horses were snorting and pawing, ready to start. They kicked up dust, while the riders reined them in, pulling back on the leather straps that held them in check.

A hush fell over the people in the audience, when they lifted their arms to acknowledge they were ready.

Shortly afterward, the signal was given, and the horses lunged forward.

Kalista's breath caught in her throat at the release of the powerful horses breaking loose from the starting line. She shouted over the roar of the crowds.

Justus clapped his hands, while turning to her. "Priscus' is flying today. It ought to be a good one without that other one in the mix."

Kalista nodded, her face registering understanding. She grinned at him.

She couldn't have been happier that Nero wasn't racing today. When that madman was on the track, it ruined the whole race. He was the worst rider, but always made sure he won, whether what he did was fair or not. The last time she'd come here to watch, he used eight horses against the others who only were allowed four. Another time, he was given a lighter cart with spiked wheels. Whatever the case, the race was always rigged.

She leaned forward, regarding the emperor. He was in a special box in the stands, sitting between highly bejeweled women with gaudy robes. Even though she could barely see him from where she sat, she knew who he was, because of his deep purple robe and the gold sash splayed across his rounded belly. He was drunk as usual, screaming at the racers on the track.

32

Kalista's Hope

She turned away, disgusted, and thrust her blue banner in the air, glad she wasn't forced to wave a purple one for him, another advantage to not having him on the track.

When the chariots rounded the first corner, the men in the low, wooden carts lashed their whips at the horses to try and gain momentum around the dusty track.

Priscus charged into the front, the shrieks from the crowd drowning out the pounding of his horse's feet.

Kalista raised her hands to her mouth calling out, when the chariot careened past the stands where they sat, the wheels of Priscus' cart whirring over ruts and uneven patches of dirt. Particles flew into the air behind all the horses, as they tore up the track past the stands multiple times.

Kalista delighted in the fact that all the horses were so closely matched throughout the duration of the race, and there was a catch in her throat when the last bronze egg in the middle of the track was lowered to show the race was almost done. The pounding of the horse's hooves only heightened the sense of excitement she felt, as the competition drew to a close.

When the last bend stretched before the lead chariots, the crowd jumped to its feet. Kalista and Justus followed suit. "Home stretch!" Her voice was becoming hoarse from yelling.

The men whipped their horses down the final lane. The top three chariots passed, all within sight of the finish line, making their way to the end.

"Force them, Priscus! Goooo!!!!!" Kalista shrieked. "I knew he'd win! He's in first place!"

Justice laughed, as the winning horse streaked toward the finish line, and the other racers strained behind him.

Suddenly, Kalista grabbed Justus' arm. She noticed Priscus' cart wobbling and shaking. The movement was slight at first, but then became more pronounced, as the racers closed in on the last lengths of the race. "Something's wrong, Justus."

"Let go. I want to see." He shrugged her off.

Kalista's eyes narrowed, and she pulled her hand away, but she was sure something had gone awry. "It's his wheel." Then, a slamming and rocking motion jarred the cart again.

Justus bent forward. He suddenly nodded. "I see what you're saying."

She gave him a look of annoyance. "I told you."

He didn't reply, but watched the cart closely.

33

Kara S. McKenzie

A screeching sound came from one of the wheels, which suddenly pitched and wobbled off its axle, then careened into the path of the horse directly behind it.

Both riders were simultaneously thrown from their perches.

The two men flew into the path of three thundering riders behind them.

Kalista watched in horror, as the other carts bounced over the bodies of the two men, delivering blows to their limp forms, chucking them into savage rolls, until they lay silent on the track.

Very suddenly, all the chariots came to a halt, and the people in the arena froze.

Kalista lifted her hand to her mouth. She'd never seen anything so horrific, so close to where she sat.

A wheel rolled past the stands making clicking sounds. It came to a stop, falling with a thud. Some of the people in the stands sat back down in their seats, and at the same time a huge groan rose from the crowd in unison.

Kalista's voice was a whisper. "Are they all right?" She couldn't take her eyes from the track where the bodies lay.

Justus didn't say anything. His mouth was open, and he was leaning forward.

One of the men got up and wobbled to the edge of the track, where he sat down, while guards flocked around him. The crowds clapped to show their relief.

Kalista was hoping Priscus would do the same, but he didn't move and remained facedown on the track.

A man who looked like a doctor ran to him and checked his breathing. After careful examination, he called out to the people in the stands, "He's dead!"

There was a hushed silence in the crowds, and then there were growing whispers as men carried the body to a chamber beneath the stands. Slaves cleared the pieces of broken chariots from the track and took the disoriented horses out of the gates. Within a short space of time, all evidence of the accident had been cleared away, and new riders were brought onto the track.

People got back in their seats and readied themselves for the next race. The solemn mood was gradually replaced with a lighthearted banter.

A lump swelled in the back of Kalista's throat. "He died."

Justus nodded.

34

Kalista's Hope

"But, Justus, they move on to the next race, as if nothing happened." Her voice quavered.

The chariots rolled back into their starting positions.

Kalista couldn't understand the lack of emotion in the people after the horses and man were taken away. She wondered what caused the death. Or whether Priscus had his own hand in it.

She laid her hand on her chest. "He might have neglected his offerings to Felicitas, or Mars? Or maybe, Janus, or one of the others?"

"Kalista."

"But, there are hundreds. No one can appease them all. It's not possible." A chill went through her. Somehow life seemed pointless, when she thought of how quickly it could be extinguished. The verses she'd read earlier, emphasized hope and new life, when the author spoke of death, and she wondered at the meaning of it. "Justus?"

He put his hand on her arm. "Let it go. We can't do anything. Look. There's another race."

She frowned. "But, I can't let it go. Someone just died, and all you're concerned with is another race?" She stared at him, her eyes wide.

"No one can understand death, Kalista. Don't even try." Justus let go of her and frowned. It was as if he wanted to shove the whole matter beneath the stands.

"But there are some who claim to understand it, and don't even seem afraid of it." She thought of what she read earlier. "The Christians even seem to welcome it."

"Christians? What made you think of them?" He frowned. "Don't listen to them."

"Well, have you ever talked to any of them?"

"No. But, I don't think it takes anyone with much sense to know they're bordering on delusional. How many gods do they have? Only one. What good is that?"

Kalista frowned. "I don't know. I don't even know where they put him?"

"And do you care?"

She twisted a lock of her hair. "I just wondered, because I never saw a cast. And they don't speak of a place to go to offer sacrifices to him."

"Kalista, it doesn't matter. It's all the same."

35

She sighed, eying the spot on the track, Priscus body was taken from. "But, do you really think so? Isn't there assurance in anything?"

Justus turned abruptly and shot her a look of warning. "Have you been talking to them?"

Kalista's face reddened. "No, I found some of their writings and was reading it. But, I don't believe any of it." She turned away, watching the carts for the second race as they rounded the first turn.

Justus sat back in his seat, relief flooding into his face. "Oh. Well, I'm glad you don't. Some are swayed by their ridiculous views, and I wouldn't want you to be. Then you'd be after me to hear it."

He reached down to retie one of the laces on his sandal that had come undone.

She laughed, a sheepish feeling sweeping over her. "Ha! I'm sure I'd be the last one to believe what they do."

She turned back to the track again, pushing the disturbing thoughts of the last race away. She wasn't going to let the death of one man, spoil the rest of her afternoon.

"It looks as if there are a few more to watch." Justus pointed to the charioteers. "And I heard Nero's playing his lyre for an audience later."

Kalista's brow moved upward. "I'm glad I didn't get an invitation." She whispered it so others wouldn't hear. "Someone said he's not any good at it."

She took another look around the stadium. She still hadn't been able to spot that man she'd met the day before in the crowded stadium. But, she knew it would be like spotting one in a million stars in the sky. She supposed she'd see him soon enough at the Christian meeting, but it wasn't exactly the place she'd want *him* to see her at. Maybe she'd find a way to watch without him knowing.

She got up from her seat and followed Justus out of the stadium.

***

Nero's out of tune voice rang out in the auditorium. His voice began to wane and crack after an hour of song.

It was probably a good time to end his serenade. He put his instrument down and finished the last notes, smiling. Although his eyes glowed with pride at the wild cheers, a sigh

Kalista's Hope

escaped his lips, and he pushed annoying thoughts to the back of his mind.

What did he care if most of the people there considered his performances unsavory for an emperor? It was something he enjoyed, and they'd surely sit for him…at least if they knew what was good for them. What harm came from such a thing? Someday, he'd make it a public performance, but for now it wasn't possible. He'd wait until the time for it was ripe.

Two slaves took hold of the massive, golden curtains on both sides of the stage, awaiting his command.

Nero stood up, bowing. The room continued to thunder with applause. He scanned the area, searching for dissenters. They'd better clap. He motioned to the slaves holding the curtains, to let them fall. He turned halfway round to the side of the stage where Poppaea was.

A grin stole over her face when their eyes met.

Nero smiled back at her, noting the sly expression on her face. She differed little from most women, using her charm and body to wend her way into power, yet behind Poppaea's beauty, there were brains in that pretty head of hers. He appreciated this aspect of her. Out of the many he'd plucked from the streets for his pleasure, he had not found one who matched Poppaea's worth. She'd a bit of a twisted side to her that appealed to him.

Poppaea lifted her chin, casting the length of her white blonde hair over her shoulders. Her green silk floated around her, as she flounced his way. "We need a plan." She smiled mischievously at him.

He was intrigued by the expression on her face. "Let's move into a more private place to talk, Poppaea." He murmured in her ear, for none to hear but her. "I sent Octavia to my mother's."

She eyed him with a mixture of seduction and distaste. "You've done well." She purred like a cat, wrapping her arm through the crook of his, leaning up against him. "I'm glad your wife's safely out of the way. Let's get out of here. We've little time to be alone together. I'm interested in what you have to tell me."

***

Nero sighed. The day was hotter than he'd expected, but at least the shade beneath the pavilion protected Poppaea and himself from it. Twelve rose-colored marble columns surrounded

37

them in a rectangular fashion, holding the platform in place above their heads.

Nero admired the patterned marble tiles, squares of olive greens, yellows and mauve, spilling out designs on the floor. The carefully placed fountains opposite them were specifically engineered for his enjoyment, which he relished in. As emperor, he loved the fact that he could have anything he wanted.

"Go!" Nero commanded slaves standing nearby. The servants in the courtyard, immediately moved to the doorways and exited through them, leaving the emperor and his mistress alone.

He eyed Poppaea curiously. "Come closer, pet. Tell me your thoughts."

Poppaea eyes glowed, as they rested on the magnificent arched stone entrances, as if reveling in their great handiwork. She took his hand in hers and turned to him. "I'm glad your mother's finally away from us. It's so much easier this way. You know she wasn't good for you, Nero."

She got up and began to pace, her brows arched. "And yet…she still has such influence with the people, even from Misenam. I assumed the riverside would be far enough away."

Nero grunted, dropping his arm to his side, the sleeve of his shimmering robe slipping over his wrist. "The riverside? Far enough for her?" He lifted a chalice of purple wine to his lips. His eyes were dark and cold. "You underestimate my mother, Poppaea. I'm disappointed in you."

After putting the container on an ornate marble stand next to him, he made another sound. "Not even the Orient would be far enough for the likes of her. Somehow that woman has a way of executing her plans, whether she's present or not. She has so much influence over the people."

Poppaea sidled up behind him, rubbing his tense shoulders with her slender fingers, her grip tightening. "You're right, you know. She'll always be a thorn in your side, whether she's near or far." The dark kohl lining in her green eyes, gave her a predatory expression, as if ready for the hunt. "So, what do you propose to do…with her?"

Nero frowned. "What do you mean?" He shook his head, not wanting to discuss the problem he knew was festering in his life. He shoved a hand through his short, blonde curls, straightening the crown on the top of his head.

Kalista's Hope

Poppaea began to take to the tiles in front of him, making feline strides back and forth, while she studied him through tapered eyes. "Well...I was thinking it might be good to send her away on a ship somewhere, or something like that, so she's in a place where she loses some of her influence." She pulled a long strand of blonde hair over her shoulder and began trailing her fingers through it.

His head bent in an arc to watch her. He liked the way she moved and how she kept her figure so trim and her soft, delicately hair so meticulously arranged. And thus far, her counsel had been sound. Life had surely gotten easier for him without that domineering mother of his around, and also Octavia, his vexatious wife, out of the way.

Poppaea quit pacing and went to him, curling up next to him. "Nero, I've had your best interests in mind since we met." Her eyes cast their catlike slant at him, and she stroked his chin with her long fingernails. "And I really don't want to get between a mother and son... but, as I said before, she's not good for you. You can't carry out your plans with her anywhere near you."

Nero tugged on a blonde tendril, falling loose from the golden, jeweled clasp in her hair and slipping over her shoulder. "You're right, sweet." A grin spread over his face. "I can't have her near me, *or* near the people who serve me, any longer."

She pushed the strand of hair behind her and slipped her hand behind his neck, raking her nails over the back of it.

He chuckled. "Hmm...a ship, you say. That just might be the answer."

He watched as she drew her hand back, and let out a pleased sound.

Her face gleamed with the thought. "There are remote islands..."

Nero put his hand up, and she stopped talking.

She watched him, curious, but with a look that told him she wasn't altogether happy, that he didn't wish to hear her idea out.

"I've an idea." A mad look came into his eye.

Poppaea frowned. "About the ship? Or something else?" She seemed concerned.

Nero held her by the neck, pulling her ear close to his lips. "That I might have one built specifically for the purpose of transporting her. It might be pleasurable to hear the herald tell news of it going down in deep waters...with her on it."

39

Poppaea's eyes positively glowed at the idea. She let go of his shoulders and scooted beside him on the bench, spreading out her golden gown around her. "Hmm." She purred like a cat. "Not a bad idea. I like it."

He feigned astonishment, but then chuckled when she looked concerned. "Don't be anxious, my dove. I like it, too."

Then he threw his head back laughing manically, amused with the thoughts racing through his head.

Poppaea sat back down, and took a sip of wine from the chalice she was holding, a vicious gleam of triumph taking hold in her.

***

Chapter 5

It had been a week since Kalista chanced to venture out alone again, after the last incident on the dark streets. She wouldn't admit it, even to herself, yet the scene she witnessed with Nero shook her confidence.

Restless and irritable as ever, there was no way she was going to miss the chance to spy on the Christians to get as much information from their secret meetings as she could. So, she made up her mind to visit the house of Narcissus, even if it was only a few hours until dusk.

After paying tribute to the gods, before leaving her residence, she set out on the stone path leading through the city. The air was cool, yet the sun streamed down, bathing Kalista in traces of warmth. She walked past neat rows of small, wooden homes with terra cotta roofs tightly jammed together on the city streets, marveling at the unique designs of each of them.

She quickened her pace, anxious to see what went on at these meetings. If this was the same Narcissus she was thinking of, she could hardly believe it. The man was senseless to get involved with such a group. The secretary of Claudius? And he wasn't capable of intellectual thought?

Earlier, she'd dressed in a simple, coarse, brown tunic with a swatch of cloth thrown over the top of her head, to attract as little attention as possible. If other women were there, and the crowd was large, she might slip into the midst of them unnoticed.

Nearing Narcissus' home, she draped the scarf protectively over her, covering most of her face. She walked up the stone path.

Narcissus home was similar to hers with a large, rectangular inner courtyard made of stone and many surrounding rooms. While men, women and children padded quietly through the wooden gateway, she slipped between them and went into the house, settling herself on a stone bench at the far end of the room.

She was careful to notice the absence of gods at the door, puzzling at people who denied tribute to them. They didn't fear Rome's deities or agonize over neglecting their duties to them? Maybe they stored them elsewhere? But, she hadn't seen evidence, and this made her uneasy.

Kara S. McKenzie

When she left her home, she brought a grain of garland to present to Mefitas, goddess of poisonous vapors, hoping the offering might prevent an untimely death. How many times had she possibly stopped something bad from happening because of her careful actions?

The soft sound of lutes played quietly in the background, while she scanned the crowd for anyone she might recognize. It wasn't long before she spied the young man she'd met the week before. He was sitting on a wooden bench near the front of the room.

Something inside her tensed when she saw him. She remembered his caring manner, and the way he spoke so tenderly to her, and she didn't understand why it made her so very uncomfortable. And yet, she supposed it had something to do with her upbringing, which didn't afford such luxuries. Domnica and her father treated her much the opposite.

She couldn't help noting the way others flocked to him, and how his manner was so relaxed and confident in the midst of their company. He seemed amused by what everyone around him was saying, and seemed to listen to the things others said with great interest.

A young woman brought bread on a tray for him and he leaned over, taking a slice from her. He said something Kalista couldn't hear, but she noticed the young woman smiling warmly at his response. Her brow drew into a frown. It seemed he had many admirers.

Hidden beneath the swatch of cloth, she had a chance to study him more closely.

As much as she wanted to distance herself from him, she also felt drawn to him for some reason. Maybe it was his encouraging manner and easy smile, or that he seemed so self-assured around so many different people? Whatever it was, she couldn't be sure.

Although, she'd noticed some of the other Christians seemed relaxed and also very responsive to others there. She wondered whether they were hiding their true thoughts, or whether they were as sincere as they seemed.

When more trays of food were brought around, Kalista broke off a piece of bread and thanked the woman serving it. She took a bite, nibbled on more bread, and took a sip of wine from the chalice she was given.

Kalista's Hope

The interactions between the people there perplexed her, by the fact that the rich and poor intermingled with each other. She couldn't believe Aristobulus, the great-grandson of Herod the Great, was spending time in rapt discussion with a man in a dark, coarse robe of the plebian class, clearly his unequal. And Aquilla, a mere tentmaker and his wife Priscilla, was with Narcissus, a favorite in the court of Nero. And here, slaves intermingled with people of the upper class. She'd never seen such closeness between people of so many different walks of life.

An older woman with eyes that crinkled at the corners, made her way across the room. She was wearing a simple, coarse linen tunic with little embellishment. "Excuse me." She bent down to Kalista. "Do you mind if I sit by you? I'm Tryphena."

Kalista was reticent to answer. She spoke quietly. "I don't mind. Please, take a seat."

The woman got down beside Kalista. "It's good to meet you."

She appeared genuine, yet Kalista only tipped her head in response. She didn't want to get too close to any of the people here or have any of them recognize her. Her father was an important man and wouldn't appreciate having his daughter connected to this group in any way.

She looked around again and couldn't help noticing on the walls, the most beautiful frescos she'd ever seen adorned with brightly colored gardens and tall, willowy trees. The room was warm and festive.

Tryphena and Kalista both turned when Narcissus strode to the front of the room. He put up his hands to start the meeting.

Kalista waited, hoping to hear something she could bring back to her father, something that showed the Christians were taking part in activities that could hurt or injure the ruling parties of Rome, any piece of evidence that might be held against them. She'd heard of their intolerance for others.

"Everyone, please. Take a seat, and we'll begin."

He spoke quietly. "Let's open in prayer and bow out of reverence to our Father God." He raised his arms.

Everyone in the room closed their eyes and lowered their heads. Kalista looked around confused, searching for any sign of the Hebrew God they were praying to, but seeing none. There were only stark white columns rising up to meet the ceiling and an occasional ornate bench and stand.

43

It was all very odd that Narcissus gave thanks and praise and then petitioned this god to speak to them, love them, and care for them, and keep them unified as one, when she saw no evidence of his existence anywhere in the room. There was no statue.

Narcissus voice cracked as if deeply touched, and he spoke with reverence for a good portion on the sundial.

Kalista searched anything false in his manner of speech or in his voice, yet she was puzzled, as she could discern no such thing. There was nothing he said that could tie him into any activities that her father might not approve of.

When the prayer ended, the old woman wiped tears from her eyes. She drew her outer wrap around her.

Kalista was prepared to offer her comfort, yet she realized it wasn't sadness that touched the woman, but joy…tears of happiness.

This was a peculiar group of people. Others there wore the same tender expressions as the woman. She tried to make sense of it.

Narcissus looked up. "Let's praise him now, with songs from our heart. Aquilla's leading."

Aquilla got up from his seat and sang, while women shook tambourines, and a man played a lute. The songs were soft and quiet, sung in reverence.

Kalista twisted in her seat. Even though others appeared deeply touched, the tune didn't particularly move her.

She found nothing in the meeting politically dangerous or anything that might lead to trouble with Rome's authorities. And as her time there was coming to a close, she lamented the fact she'd have nothing to tell her father. She wondered if these people had a hidden agenda and were growing their forces, holding back for the purposes of keeping their plans undercover.

When the music ended, she inclined her head, paying close attention to the elderly man who spoke.

His words stirred emotions, inspiring enthusiastic nods and tender smiles from the people there. And yet, Kalista frowned at the fact his message was about compliance and living in peace with others, despite their differences, without conforming to or taking part in things that were not in agreement with their beliefs.

She was surprised when Aquilla started speaking to them about the treatment of women, and how the men should focus on

Kalista's Hope

love and respect toward them. He made it clear that dominance and control was never a good thing, and that Jesus wanted them to care deeply for others and put women first. He said that, in this way, the women might give themselves freely in trust to the men they loved.

Kalista was confused the men believed this way about women. Yet, by the approving nods and the wide grins in the room, she realized these Christian men did.

She stood when the speech ended, and then realized they meant to pray again, so abruptly sank back down in her seat. She nudged the woman next to her. "Typhena? Where's the god? I don't see him."

"Wait, and I'll tell you after the prayer."

When Aquilla was finished, Kalista suddenly felt very out of place. Something in this room made her tense and anxious. She decided she'd not wait around for Typhena's answer. A chill crept over her, and she pulled the folds of her outer wrap around her.

She sprang from her seat. "I'm sorry, but it's getting late, and I need to be going." She placed a hand on Typhena's shoulder. "I'll hear it another time."

"But…" The woman reached out to her.

"No…I have to go." Kalista cringed a bit at her lie, yet stole away into the crowd and left the room, shaking off an ominous feeling inside. Within minutes, she was on the path toward her home. It was approaching evening, but luckily Palantine Hill was not far.

***

Making her way down the trail, Kalista shivered from the cold. The air around her smelled dank and earthy. Long shadows fell at angles from the homes, as statue gods seemed to guard the path along the edge of the road. Darkness would come quickly. She pulled her headscarf around her, clutching it tightly in her fist.

She let out a slow breath, thinking back to the meeting and the people there, wishing she'd not gone. She couldn't seem to put their incessant music to rest in her head. A line about a great god and the love they shared, kept drumming like madness within her. The disturbing lyrics hung around her like an unwanted vendor.

45

She heard footsteps behind her, but before she could turn back, a hand gently tugged on her tunic and then lifted the scarf off her head. "Kallie?"

It was the young man who had brought her home the week before. He held her wrap in his hand. His hair was in disarray, and he looked a bit winded from chasing her down.

Kallie smelled a musk-like scent from the incense at the home they were at. She backed away from him, staring at him disconcerted.

The line in her brow deepened, and she spoke quietly. "Remember. I told you, it's Kalista."

He smiled, nonplussed with her answer. "You told me, you didn't care what I called you." And then he winked, his eyes crinkling at the corners. "I didn't think it mattered."

Something tugged inside Kalista as she stood watching him. His smile was so warm and inviting. And she couldn't help admiring his openness. And yet, he was almost too kind. So much so, it made her wary.

So, instead of engaging him in a likewise manner, she shrugged instead and turned away, looking down the street. "I suppose I did tell you this, fair enough. Call me what you like."

She turned back, noticing the dark ring beneath his eye from when she last took a swipe at him. She lifted her hand to her mouth in surprise, and then quickly regained her composure. "You know you shouldn't sneak up behind me. I was very close to striking you, again. You must watch what you're doing."

He laughed and then without pause, he leaned down, whispering in her ear. "I think I told you it would be a black eye." His look was playful and teasing.

Her breath caught slightly at his nearness, and she felt her face grow warm. She pushed him away, taking her scarf back from him. "You said it would be, and you're right. But, it's not so bad. And is healing."

He laughed. "Well, it is better, now. But it's been a bit difficult to explain to my friends, and I've had to take quite a bit of taunts over it."

She couldn't help a slight smile. "I suppose you have. But, it was dark, and I didn't know you."

"This is true. And I can't fault you for it."

He stopped walking and took her arm, holding her back a moment. His eyes were suddenly full of questions. "I saw you in

Kalista's Hope

the back of the room, at Narcissus' home. I've not seen you there before. Why were you were at the meeting?"

She tipped her chin up. "You knew I was there? Why didn't you speak to me then?"

"I didn't know it was you, at first. But, at the end, I noticed you, talking to Tryphena. After you stood to leave, I noticed your hair under your scarf." He tugged on a strand. "And it's not difficult to miss in a crowd."

Her cheeks burned. She moved down the path, not wishing to be reminded of Domnica and Camila's latest comments. She wrapped her scarf back over her head, tying it behind her and tucking the strands beneath.

"Kallie? I didn't mean to offend you. Wait a minute." He caught up with her on the path and strode alongside. "It's very pretty. I like it."

She looked away, not accustomed to compliments. She didn't quite know what to say. Her eyes trailed the road. "I hope you didn't think I needed an escort again, because I can walk back without anyone."

She glanced at him, annoyed by the fact that her comments didn't seem to deter him in anyway. She couldn't help admiring his persistence, despite the fact that she was trying her best to discourage him.

He smiled. "I'm sure you can get back on your own. But, I don't mind."

Then, he repeated his earlier question. "So, why did you come to our meeting?"

She stopped suddenly. She twisted the ends of her scarf, not wanting to tell him the truth, especially after finding out nothing was gained by going there. Did he have to delve into everything she did?

"Well, if you must know, it wasn't to see you." The words came out more abruptly than she intended, and immediately she felt contrite. "I mean. I had other reasons."

He looked amused, and he moved with her as she began to walk again. "But, how did you know about it? Were you at the last one?"

She shrugged. "I read a note a boy dropped outside the Gates of Janus, and I had questions." She lifted her tunic to step over an uneven section of the path.

He eyed her more closely. "Hmm. So, why didn't you say anything when we met, or at the meeting?"

47

Kara S. McKenzie

A guilty look crossed her face. "I don't know. I just wondered about the Christians and their beliefs, and didn't want to talk to anyone about it."

He took her arm, scrutinizing her. "But, you could have said something. Instead, you dressed in clothes you clearly didn't want to be recognized in and kept this scarf over your head while you were there. For some reason, I don't think your going there, had anything to do with you wanting to learn more about our faith."

It grated her that he was right, and she didn't like it one bit. "And why wouldn't I? You don't think I could? I suppose you don't think I'm good enough for something like that?" She shrugged him off.

Her eyes narrowed, and something suddenly brewed like poison inside her. No one thought much of her. And she knew if he was around her for long, he wouldn't either, she was sure.

"Kallie." He pushed his hand through his hair. "None of us are good enough on our own. You gave indications that your beliefs were different, and I didn't think you'd be interested. I'm willing to help you learn if you'd like?"

Know more about the Christian beliefs? She didn't think so. She waved her hand at him. "I've seen enough. No, you don't need to show me anything."

Then he stopped, as if a thought occurred to him. "The first time we met, you told me you recognized me, then you changed your mind?"

She was unsure of what to say, so she lied. "I don't remember." She looked at her feet, and then realizing they were dirty, tucked them under her tunic.

He smiled, a light in his eyes. "But, it's true. I heard you. You did recognize me. I know it."

She pursed her lips, not saying anything. It disturbed her to no end that he seemed to be able to read her mind.

When he leaned closer to her, tipping up her chin, she quickly backed away, her eyes wide. She didn't understand the flutter she felt inside her, but it made her hesitant and wary of him.

And then it was if he suddenly knew the answer. He laughed. "You were spying…for your father? I'm right, aren't I?"

She flicked her hair from her eyes, but didn't look at him. "That's ridiculous. I wasn't spying." It irritated her to no end

48

Kalista's Hope

that he seemed to have this clairvoyance about her and then made a joke of it.

He laughed again. "You were! That's it!"

She clasped her hands together, twisting them as she spoke. "I only wanted to see. They said you were starting rebellions."

"And you believe the people there tonight were violent or capable of such things?"

Kalista wished she wouldn't have gone to the ridiculous meeting in the first place. She wouldn't have had to explain herself to him if she hadn't. "Well, I don't know…" She fumbled for his name, but still didn't know it.

"It's Gaius." The blue in his eyes was clear, and there was a spark in them. "My name, that is."

"Oh." She fixed her eyes on the path, not looking at him.

"I live across the city from you."

He matched her stride. "You know your parents should be more watchful of you. It's going to be late soon, and like I said, you shouldn't be alone. How old are you, anyway?"

"Old enough. I'll be seventeen. But, I didn't choose the time for this meeting."

He was suddenly serious. "Seventeen." He raked a hand through his hair. "Your age is exactly the reason you shouldn't be out here without a guardian."

She sighed. "Why has this become the topic of everyone I talk to, lately? I think there's some kind of conspiracy to keep me chained to the house."

Her scarf fell off, and she took it in her hand, letting her bright red hair tumble freely down her back. There was so much of it, but she refused to cut it, as she'd been told it was a likeness of her mother.

Gaius stared open-mouthed at the long strands and took a step closer. He reached out and pushed a wayward piece of her hair back from her face, studying her expression.

Kalista couldn't deny that he liked what he saw and was puzzled by it. She took a step back, pretending not to notice, and persisting in her complaint. "Well, if anyone else tries to trap me inside that house again, I'll scream."

He eyed her curiously, and then smiled. "I suppose you were right. You'd no choice when it came to the meeting time. So, I'll walk back the rest of the way with you, because it's partly due to me that you're here."

49

Kara S. McKenzie

Kalista sighed. Deep down, as much as she felt uncertain around Gaius, she was glad she wouldn't be alone when the sun went down. She could see Palentine Hill from where they were, and it looked as if the games were going on in the Coliseum near the hill. Plumes of dust were rising above it, and the roar of the crowds escaped its many arched doorways. It wouldn't be long before the people there would be on the streets, rowdy and drunken as usual.

She shrugged, wanting him to think it mattered little to her whether he stayed or went. "Do what you want."

Then, her mind shifted to what she read in the letter from Paul.

As long as Gaius was going to insist on walking the rest of the way with her, maybe he could help her clear up a few things. There were a few things she still didn't understand in the writings she found. "I found one of Paul's letters."

Gaius' eyes widened slightly. "And read it?"

She nodded.

"So, what did you think?"

"Not a whole lot. But, I wasn't sure what he meant by some things he said."

He looked curious. "Maybe I can help."

She stopped walking. "Well, when I saw you praying tonight, I wondered why there was no god in the room. In Paul's letter, he talks about a god, but I can't ever get a good picture in my mind as to what he looks like. And I can't figure out where his statue is."

Her cheeks warmed at the thought of sounding unintelligent, and yet she really wanted to understand. She pointed to the statues along the path. "I've never seen him anywhere, and don't even know his name."

"*A* god? Kallie, he's not like that." Gaius didn't seem quite sure what to say at first.

"What do you mean?"

He shrugged and looked over the horizon. "He's not just *a* god, but the one true God who made the world and everything in it."

Kalista bit her lip.

Gaius was matter of fact. "We Romans have created our own gods to control our destiny. But, this God wasn't made with human hands. He made us."

50

Kalista's Hope

Kalista shivered, knowing she'd never tried to appease this God. And yet, if there was no form, how could she?

Gaius gestured to the sky. "He made the world and everything in it, including you, evidence of who he is. Just look around. Did you ever see anything so beautiful?" He extended his arm to the expanse of hills in front of them.

She turned and looked out over the horizon. The sun was setting in the distance over Rome, weaving colors of purple and dark blue across the expanse. The great hills rose majestically behind stonewalls surrounding the city, while the first stars were making their appearance overhead. She heard the sound of birds calling to each other and smelled the scents of fresh lilies.

"He gave everything to us. And there's not one artist who could ever carve a deity so wonderful or excellent as he is." Gaius stared at the lit canopy of stars above them.

"A god like this would be powerful."

Gaius stopped walking. "He is. And, Kallie, as I said, he's the one true God, not made of stone, or silver or gold, or fashioned by human hands. He did the fashioning. And he's jealous of all the human gods we've worshipped."

She shivered, wondering how she could stand before a god like this.

Gaius eyes softened toward her. "But, he's loving, too."

She squeezed her scarf in her hands, uncomfortable with the things he was saying. She'd never be good enough for this god. "Please, don't say anymore. I don't want to hear it."

"I'm only telling you what I know and believe."

"But, I don't want it, none of it. It's what I don't like about Christians, shoving beliefs on everyone." She sighed. "I should've walked alone."

Gaius was silent on the path up the hill. As they neared Kalista's father's estate, he pushed aside an overhanging branch on the walk to clear the way for her.

Kalista ducked under it, while he held it for her.

It bothered her that he treated her with kindness, even when she didn't deserve it. She'd asked him about his religion, then got upset with him for telling her.

Her stomach suddenly felt like knots inside her, and she couldn't think straight. Gaius didn't despise her as her family did, even when she disagreed with him. He treated her with respect, despite her harsh words. He was a puzzle to her, different from anyone she'd ever encountered.

51

Kara S. McKenzie

When they reached her family's home, she lifted the latch to the gate to let herself into the courtyard. She turned back, eyeing him warily. "My father and stepmother say I've a wicked tongue. I'm sure I was born with it."

Gaius studied her for a moment, then, touched her arm, gently chiding her. A sparkle lit in his eyes. "So, you're apologizing?"

Kalista drew back. "I never said...."

He smiled, laying his fingers to her lips, stopping her in mid-sentence. His eyes were kind and sympathetic. "It's all right. I know what you meant."

She sighed, a look of resignation in her eyes.

They continued up the path in silence, until they reached a back door of her home.

"I hope you'll at least think about my God." He took hold of her hand. "I know he *can* help you, if you'd only go to him. He loves you very much."

She let go of him, affected deeply by the things he said. She was perplexed. She choked back a sob forming in her throat. There was a tender side emanating from him, she couldn't begin to understand, and didn't know if she wanted to.

"Don't say more." She said it, as tears formed in her eyes. Gaius had a troubling effect on her. Her heart was beginning to quicken its beat, and her stomach felt weak. She turned, waving him off as she walked away from him.

"Kallie."

She heard his voice again behind her and stopped in her tracks. She was only half intent on hearing what he had to say. She pushed down a rising feeling of dread inside her and whirled around to face him.

He didn't say anything at first, and then looked at her as if he was unsure about whether or not to continue. "You might stop running."

She shook her head, an odd questioning look in her eyes. "I don't know what you mean, running?" And then, she put up her hand, not wanting to hear his answer. She'd had enough for one day. "Please, I have to go inside. It's night, and we're at my home."

Gaius reached out to her. "Running from me, and from others. And from the fear you have."

52

Kalista's Hope

Some of the things he said made her feel as if she were on the defense. She waved his hand away. "That's ridiculous. Fear? You don't know what you're talking about."

Gaius looked her square in the eye. "Rather than hide, you should face it."

Something he said struck deep inside Kalista. He couldn't know anything, or how she felt. He'd only known her a short time. But, she had a bad feeling about his words of advice, ones she could well do without. "I said I wasn't running from anything. Now, I have to go. It's late."

She heard him from behind. "Just pray, Kallie. He'll help you."

She bristled. She wasn't used to anyone showing care or concern for her wellbeing. It was probably one of the things she feared most in her life. There were many things welling up inside her, and she didn't feel comfortable sharing with others, especially strangers.

She suddenly jerked away and bolted toward the house, not understanding why she felt the way she did, but wanting to escape. She called out to him. "I don't need anyone to tell me how I feel."

And when she reached the door, she added over her shoulder. "And don't need your God."

She heard Gaius call to her again, but she didn't look back.

The door slammed behind her. Kalista took quick steps down the marble hallway to her room and sat down on her bed, resting her head in her hands.

Then, she lay down on her pillow, trying to quiet the beating of her heart and calm the thoughts running through her head. She felt tears welling up in her eyes, trying desparately to hold them back. She couldn't cry. If she did, she might not be able to stop. And she didn't want that kind of hurt.

It angered her that Gaius managed to break through the barrier she'd put up for others. She felt rattled inside because of it. She didn't like hearing about the Christian God and didn't want to again.

She turned to the wall, putting her hand to her chest. She squeezed her eyes shut, trying to still her heart and calm her breaths. Morning could not come soon enough, as far as she was concerned.

53

Kara S. McKenzie

***

Chapter 6

"Get up, Kalista. We're leaving." Nona popped her head in the door. "Grab an outer wrap. The streets are brisk this morning."

Kalista rubbed her eyes and put down the book she was reading. "Leaving? Where?"

"Your father needs new slaves, one for you, and one to replace the head seamstress."

"You can't get them yourself?" The business of buying slaves always sickened Kalista. Although it was accepted in Rome and other places in the world, for some reason, she never really felt comfortable with it. None of the slaves had done anything to deserve the place they were in. They were either captured or taken from their families and homes against their will, sometimes sold by those they loved, or were orphans taken from the streets.

When she went to the sale, she knew she'd see things she didn't want to see. She couldn't imagine others judging her based on her physical appearance, checking her teeth or raking their hands through her hair to examine the thickness of it. It had to be humiliating for them.

Nona limped through the doorframe and knelt by the bed. She whispered to Kalista. "Your father told me to go with Domnica if you were busy. But, both of the slaves are being purchased to keep you dressed and clean. Do you want *her* to pick them for you?"

Kalista groaned. She could only imagine the slave Domnica would choose. "No. I couldn't bear anyone she'd get for me."

"Well, that's why I came to you first."

Kalista nodded. "I suppose I should thank you for it then. Is the seamstress to replace Abigail?"

"Yes, her eyes are bad, and she can't do it anymore. She's a laundress now."

"Well, that's good for her. So, what do we need another one for?"

"To keep you bathed and dressed properly from now on."

Kalista snorted. "Surely, Domnica is behind this. Yet, she'll have no part in choosing anyone for me." She was glad Nona had come to her first.

"Yes, miss." Nona's eyes brightened.

"I'll get ready, and we'll go." She let out a breath, not exactly jumping up from her seat.

Nona breathed a sigh of relief. "Apollo Casca has slaves for sale. If we get there early enough, we might get the best of the lot. He treats his slaves better, so you'll be spared from some of the things you don't like to see."

Kalista grabbed a shawl and pitched it over her shoulder. "Thanks. I'll take my bath and meet you at the door after a visit to the household gods."

Nona bent her head in acquiescence and hobbled out, leaving Kalista to get ready.

***

Although it was still early morning and the sun had barely risen, the marketplace was teeming with people. The slaves Apollo Casca intended to sell, were fully clothed, standing behind stone blocks with a wax stylus out, detailing past records and family history. Right away, Kalista read the wax tablets for a tall, dark-haired woman.

"She looks efficient and can sew."

Nona shook her head.

The woman's eyes sparkled despite her circumstances. Her sleek, dark hair slipped over her shoulder, and she tossed it behind her. Her shoulders were back, her posture straight. Something about her told Kalista she'd not be the typical slave Domnica would've bought, cowering and subservient. Her name was listed as Chaya, a Jewess, yet she could speak Latin and Greek.

"How did you end up here?"

The woman answered with no pretense or malice. "Sold..." she hesitated. "By my sisters."

Her appearance was flawless, her tunic neat and clean. A simple necklace draped about her slightly elongated neck. The amulet swinging from it, matched the amber color of her eyes.

Her sisters did this? Kalista knew if Camila had her way, she, herself would have been auctioned off a long time ago, for a bronze coin or two, without a backward glance.

She frowned. The only reason she was still in the home was because of her father, and that wasn't saying much.

56

Kalista's Hope

"Take her, Nona. Tell them to put the bill on my father's account."

Nona nodded, then limped to where Apollo's servants were turning over documents and handling the sales.

Kalista swiveled around when she heard laughter.

A young Greek woman surrounded by children, was playfully teasing them. Her dark, wavy hair was tied back loosely and kept falling from its clasp. She retied it, while the children giggled around her. One of them reached out and tugged her jingling ankle bracelets, and she pulled her sandaled foot away quickly, smiling.

Kalista was intrigued by the young woman's enthusiasm, not hindered by her situation. She read the stylus on the platform next to her and spoke to one of Apollo's servants. "How do you say her name?"

When the servant didn't turn around, the woman answered. "Ta-see-a. I'm Greek." She smoothed back her hair, the bracelet on her arm making noise as it slipped clumsily down her arm. She held it tight to her wrist.

"What's your background?"

The slave's eyes flickered. "My mother was from Rome. I was seventeen. My father died before I knew him, and my mother later. I'm twenty now. I was a woman's personal attendant, but she's no longer living."

Kalista witnessed a flash of hurt in Tasia's eyes when she talked about losing her parents and ignored the stab of pain that tore through her own chest. She felt the urge to draw back and look for a different slave, and then she remembered what Gaius said to her about her running from things.

Her lips tightened. She took the stylus from the stand next to Tasia and quickly read through it. "You'll do. My father wants someone to attend to my needs."

Tasia dipped her head, her eyes producing a spark. "Oh, thank you!"

Kalista smiled. Tasia wasn't exactly what Domnica would have in mind, a bit exuberant for what her stepmother would have chosen. But she, on the other hand, thought Tasia was perfect.

Nona came back with Chaya at her side. "She's paid for." She studied the young Greek girl standing next to Kalista. "You're not picking her, are you?"

"I think she'd be good."

57

Kara S. McKenzie

Tasia hopped from one foot to the other, the bells jingling on her ankles. She smoothed out her tunic, her unruly hair falling forward.

"Does she have any experience?"

Kalista nodded. "She was a personal attendant to a woman for three years."

Nona gave her a sidelong glance.

"I know she isn't what you were thinking, but I've made up my mind. I want her." Kalista sighed, not exactly reveling in the fact that she was purchasing a slave.

"I see. I only hope Domnica won't take me to task for bringing her back."

"I won't let her. I'm not afraid of her."

"The Jewess will suffice, yet the Greek would be more suited to a household with a little less propriety. Domnica wants societal rules to be met, and this Tasia will have difficulty conforming to her standards."

"I know, but it's not for her to decide." Kalista stared fixedly ahead.

Nona looked worried, but sighed resignedly. "I see I'll not change your mind."

"No, she's who I want." Kalista smiled. After speaking with Nona, she was even more sure Tasia would be a good choice. The woman was exactly what she was looking for.

They paid for Tasia and left the marketplace, both slaves trailing behind.

***

Kalista laughed when Chaya and Tasia stepped through the doorway of their new home. Both their eyes widened at the towering walls of white with massive columns holding up the roof, the décor ornate, to the point of being overdone.

"Don't be afraid. Unless Domnica's near, you can speak freely here."

Tasia was hesitant, then brightened when she realized Kalista was serious. "Everything is huge, and the frescos are so beautiful and rich."

"Yes. My stepmother hasn't learned the art of sparing my father's coins on lavish furnishings." Kalista's tone was dry, and there was an agitated look on her face.

Tasia lowered her head. "I'm sorry. I didn't mean to upset you."

Kalista's Hope

"Oh, no." Kalista put up her hand. "I said what I meant. You can say what you think around me."

Tasia nodded. She still seemed unsure, but brightened at the prospect.

They followed Kalista across ancient Persian rugs, and past white, marble hallways to the inner rooms. Other slaves in the household went about their tasks, eying Tasia and Chaya curiously.

"Nona, take Chaya with you and get her settled. Tasia will come with me."

Tasia couldn't hide her displeasure at being separated from her new friend and lowered her head.

Kalista patted her shoulder. "You'll join her later and share quarters near my room. Nona has to introduce her to the staff working under her."

Tasia breathed a sigh of relief. "Oh, thank you."

"You'll be treated well here. Don't worry."

Kalista brought the slave into a small room off her quarters. "This'll be your room to share with Chaya. I hope it'll be enough." There were two straw mattresses, one in each corner.

Tasia did a little dance and flopped down on the cot. She squealed. "It's better than anything I've ever known." Her eyes filled with tears and trickled down her cheeks, and then she sat up abruptly. "Oh, I'm sorry. It's just not what I was expecting."

Kalista rolled her eyes. "Don't worry. But, you needn't show such enthusiasm over a small pallet and nightstand."

"Forgive me, again." Tasia lifted her hands to her face.

"It's near eve. Lie down. Morning comes soon enough, and you'll have duties then. Domnica won't be so lenient."

She watched as Tasia wiped tears from her eyes and settled into her pallet, curling under a woolen throw folded at the end of the bed.

"I'll talk to you tomorrow and let you know what I expect."

***

Kalista sat down on a bench in the garden in the back of her home. Flowers were in full bloom, and statues around the grounds were covered with vines. She breathed in the strong scent of the lilies in rows next to her and watched the sun setting in the west, spraying swatches of purples and pinks across the expanse of the sky. She wondered if what Gaius told her was

59

true. Could the god he spoke of have made such things? And how did they come to be, if not?

She had an unsettled feeling about the newest slave she'd purchased. Whatever possessed her to have chosen the Greek woman? The slave certainly brought with her sorrow from her past, nothing Kalista wanted to be a part of.

She hoped she could keep her temper at bay with the woman. She wasn't comfortable when dealing with emotional outbursts of any kind.

At least in this household, the slave wouldn't be beaten or mistreated, as she might be somewhere else. She and Chaya would have plenty to eat and friendships with the other slaves. There was a thread of civility in their home, regardless of Domnica and her overbearing ways.

Civility, she grimaced. From what she heard at the markets, common courtesy was losing its grips on the city. The last piece of information she gleaned from Nona, was that Nero tried to drown his mother on a sinking ship. Somehow, Agrippina managed to swim ashore and survive. Kalista couldn't fathom it.

She studied the statue in front of her, depicting a mother and a child who resembled each other. She fingered the long red strands of hair that fell over her shoulder in waves. Regardless of bloodlines, Kalista was saddened by the fact that she probably had little else in common with the elegant lady who was her mother. They may have had the same fiery colored hair, yet Kalista knew she wasn't the beauty her mother had been. And though others loved her mother for her benevolent nature, Kalista knew her own heart wasn't so good. She was not kind to others, and didn't even know how to show love.

A crisp, dry wind made her shiver, and she wrapped the shawl she brought outside with her around her shoulders, getting up from the bench to go back inside. Lately, she had too much time to think. She needed to find something to do to take her mind from things. Maybe tomorrow she'd look for a diversion.

***

"The ship didn't sink?" Poppaea moaned. She rose from her seat and took quick steps over the decorative leaf patterns on the stone floor and stood in front of the window. She looked over the view of the city from the lush hillside palace.

Nero moved behind her, frustrated. "She swam ashore in her tunic." He raked his hand through his thick hair, agitated. "How she seems to manage escape, I can't imagine."

Kalista's Hope

Poppaea whirled about. "Maybe it's time for you to take drastic measures. Drowning didn't seem to do the trick."

Nero looked annoyed. "Drastic? As in what?" He eyed her with interest, clearly attentive to her newest scheme.

"You want her out of your life, don't you?" Poppaea's green eyes narrowed.

Nero shook his head. "She won't stop meddling in my business."

Poppaea shrugged. "So, do something else, then." She dragged her fingernails along the edge of his sleeve. "You can't keep letting her get in the way of what you want. You *are* the emperor."

Nero moaned and flung his arms wide. "And yet, she's my mother, Poppaea."

Poppaea leaned up against him, her soft, red gown delicate to the touch. "I understand your allegiance toward her, dearest. It's only natural. And yet, you're a man, Nero. There comes a time when it's sometimes necessary to cut the ties, especially when it's a threat to your power and position. The people are sympathizing with *her*."

He nodded, but didn't seem sure. "I suppose you're right. And I might be able to rid myself of Octavia, if she were gone, along with some of those maddening advisors of hers."

Poppaea leaned closer to him, caressing him, as she confided in his ear. "I know an assassin who would take care of it for you. No one would need to know who sent him. You'd never have to worry again about an overthrow manipulated by her."

"An assassin?"

"It's no different than trying to drown her. It won't be by your hands, and the job would be done quickly. If left to her devices, you'll eventually lose your place as emperor. I'm sure she's plotting to depose you at this very minute."

Nero let out a breath. "I suppose you're right, but it's not something I can do without apprehension. Her people have infiltrated every secret place in my life, and I feel exposed."

"I'll speak with my friend," Poppaea cooed. She touched the sleeve of his robe and then latched him to her. "Don't worry. I'll be here for you, Nero. Once it's done, you'll feel better."

***

61

Chapter 7

People crowded into the Theater of Marcellus taking their seats. They were full of wine and raucous laughter. There was barely standing room during the opening performances. Along with clangs of Cymbals and tambourines, a woman on the stage recited parts of the Iliad by Homer.

The audience roared, hurling things at the wooden platform.

Kalista wondered what she was doing here with her stepsister. She didn't even like Camila, and they rarely did anything together. But since she had to stay in the women's section at the theater, and couldn't sit with Justus, she supposed going with her stepsister was better than being there alone.

Lately, the performances seemed less than entertaining and sometimes even tasteless and crude. She didn't know if she were changing, or if the acts were. She used to come to these places to escape Domnica, but now, she wasn't so sure it was much better.

And Gaius' words kept niggling at her. No matter where she went, she couldn't seem to escape the things he had said. He brought to mind something she'd never considered, and still wasn't prepared to admit openly. She knew she *did* run from things that caused her pain. And yet, she tried to fill her life doing things to block out what she didn't want to face. And the fact that he knew this was disconcerting to her.

A drunken soldier slumped across Kalista, while she waited for slaves to bring her and Camila food to eat during the performance.

She yelled at him. "Get off of me, you idiot! Don't you know who I am, you clumsy fool?" She shoved the man into two other people in front of her.

The crowd around them howled with laughter as the soldier got up and staggered away.

Camila smacked her on the arm. "Watch it! It's a good thing that man was as drunk as he was."

Kalista snorted. "He better not put hands either of us. Father would be angry." She was disgusted by the man's bothersome behavior and the disregard he showed for everyone around him.

Kalista's Hope

"Father?" Camila laughed. "You believe he cares what happens to *you*?"

Kalista frowned, yet said nothing, knowing her stepsister was probably right. Her father wouldn't care what anyone did to her.

Kalista tipped her head, straining to hear the slave on the stage. "If these ridiculous drunks would shut their mouths, we might hear the act we came for."

"If you wanted to hear them, you should've known you'd be disappointed. I came for the food and to watch them make fools of themselves." Camila got a wry smile on her face, tipping her head to the side.

"Well, I needed to get out of the house. I wanted nothing to do with what's going on there. They're making clothes and dreaming up hairstyles for me. And there's no way I'm going to sit around there and be a part of it. But, I didn't come to watch people stagger around in the stands either, pawing all over each other. Half of them here don't even know what they're doing."

She fixed her eyes on the woman on the stage, then watched a man get up from his seat and launch wine from his chalice onto the woman's white stola, turning it to spotted crimson. The man yelled at her. "Take it off! It's soiled now!" He staggered in the stands.

The woman on the stage ignored him and kept reading from the book she was holding.

The audience roared with laughter. Camila joined in.

"Take it off!" He bellowed again. "We didn't come to hear you read!"

Other men got up next to him and began to chant.

Kalista rolled her eyes, scowling. "They need to leave her alone. Why do they do this? She doesn't want to do what they say." She couldn't understand some of the men with their obnoxious behavior.

Camila flicked a length of her soft, blonde hair over her shoulder. "You're the one who wanted to come." She gave a bored look.

The woman on the stage shrieked, "I'm reading the Iliad and not doing what you say!"

A hush fell over the room, and the crowd stared at the audacity of the slave.

"Great." Kalista made a face. "Now she's made trouble for herself. She's not a free woman."

63

Kara S. McKenzie

The man growled. "Not? You said, not?" A red stain traveled down his cheek, and he clenched his fist. "But, you don't make that decision and do as we say!"

The woman's hands trembled, and the book fell from them. "I didn't ask to perform. There wasn't a choice."

"But you'll do it, and our way!"

The crowd began to screech again. "Off! Off! Off!"

The man staggered up on the stage from a flight of stairs, coming at her. "I said! Take it off."

She backed away.

The crowd laughed. "Throw her off! Throw her down!"

Someone else yelled. "Over the side!"

The woman bolted from the man on the stage, but before she could get far, he lunged for her arm and dragged her to the edge, giving her a great shove and toppling her over. She fell a distance and slammed down hard onto the stonework below with a loud thud.

Camila chuckled at first, and then after watching the man on the stage, she suddenly snorted. "Why does it always have to be a woman?" She bristled, clearly annoyed. "Why can't we ever see them do that to one of the male slaves?"

Kalista was irritated by the comment. "They shouldn't do it to anyone."

When the woman didn't get up, a drunken man went to the motionless body. "She should've listened, if she wanted to read the Iliad so bad!" He started to chuckle, holding his large waist.

Roaring laughter swept over the room, and others were brought onto the stage.

One of the men hollered loudly. "Toss the book! No more reading!"

Kalista threw her hands in the air. Before she left home with Camila, she looked forward to the night. She always thought things would be different. And yet, it was never the way she imagined it to be. "I've seen enough. I want to go. If I could do anything to get back at those men, I would."

"But...I wanted..."

Kalista shot out of her seat, forcing her way out of the stands. She made up her mind not to go to another of these performances.

64

Kalista's Hope

Camila reluctantly followed behind. "You shouldn't go there with such expectations," She pursed her lips. "They always treat the slaves like that, and they always get drunk."

Kalista frowned. "But it's not right. Don't you see it? And yet, some things never seem to change."

As she passed the woman on the bottom floor lying dead, bruised and bloodied, she couldn't help wondering what the point of life was, if the end came in such a way, so suddenly.

When they got back to the house, Camila turned. "Don't ever ask me to go with you again, if you can't stomach it. I would've went with Corvina, if I knew we'd have to leave so early."

Kalista rolled her eyes. "Remind me next time, and I'll stay home. Anyone who can callously watch that type of show and not bat an eyelash, isn't someone I want to go with anyway."

Camila laughed. "Good luck. You'll have trouble finding anyone like that in this city."

Kalista headed down the hall to her room, trying to push the image of the latest acceptable murder from her mind. The sad thing was, Camila was right.

And then she thought of Gaius. She supposed there were some decent people left in Rome. Not that she wanted to spend time with any of them, either.

***

Chapter 8

Kalista knelt in front of Janus, offering sweet cakes again. She rose early the next morning before any of the slaves woke.

She poured sweet perfume on the base of the statue, waiting for a response. The stone foundation felt like chalk beneath her fingertips, pieces of it chipping away. What would Janus look like years from now after the sun, wind and rain beat it down and wore it away? Did the god have any power over the elements?

A voice from behind startled her. "I wondered if you'd be here."

"Justus?" She swung round, her eyes wide. "Gaius?" Where had he come from? She stood beside him.

He looked at the two-headed god. "You come here often?"

Her eyes traveled up the clean, smooth lines of the soldier god, heads facing both east and west. She nodded, then sighed. "I figure if any of them can provide answers, he'll be it."

The statue's expression was stern, almost angry, as he scanned the horizon waiting for the man with courage who would someday come.

Gaius smiled. "So, when do you think he'll finally shut his gates?"

"You know about Janus?" She eyed him curiously, wondering what he might have to say about the god. He seemed to have a lot to say regarding topics of religion.

He shrugged. "I'm Roman, and my parents weren't Christian when I was young. I know more than you think."

She looked up at Janus. "So, you've heard the writers say that when the brave, wise man comes, who loves the people more than wealth and popularity and conquers the minds of men, then the gates will be shut for good. Only then, will the wars stop and peace prevail."

"I've heard that." He smiled. Then he pushed back a length of hair that had fallen across his forehead. There was a sparkle in his eyes.

"You're making fun of me?" Kalista gripped the edge of her gown.

Kalista's Hope

He reached out and took her hand. "Of course not. It's only that I know the man. And that he's already been here. You don't have to keep waiting any longer, Kallie."

Kalista withdrew her hand from his and backed away. "But, that's wrong. The brave, wise man hasn't come. Everyone is still waiting." What was he talking about? Did he ever make any sense at all? Nothing he said seemed to be easy to understand.

"No, not true. He has. And he's brought the peace you speak of, too."

She shook her head. "You're joking?"

He stepped closer to her. "No. You remember hearing about Jesus?" He looked out beyond the gates. "The one who came, not too long ago?"

Kalista stared at him puzzled. "Jesus? No. He isn't the one. The gates are still open, and none of this has been spoken of in Rome." She turned to the city. "And I'm not seeing the peace say is happening. The wars never end." Only yesterday, she'd watched troops marching out of the gates. He'd be crazy to believe such a thing.

Gaius put his hand on his chest. "The gates are shut for me. The peace is in here. And anyone can find the same, if they look outside the gates."

She took a step toward him, and then stopped. What he was saying didn't make any sense. It wasn't possible, outside the gates? "No. You're lying. I don't believe you. There wasn't any man, and never a speck of peace since before I was born. You're saying it was Jesus, but have nothing to base it on."

Gaius shook his head. "What reason would I have to lie?"

She met his clear, bluish gray eyes. Her hand brushed against the base of Janus, and she shivered, the stone cold against her fingers. Fear coursed through her at the thought of displeasing the war god. "Your religion doesn't make sense."

He sighed. "And your statue gods do nothing for you." He lifted his hand to the sky. "But, a living breathing one, who loves you more deeply than you can imagine, can." His expression tore at her heart, a genuine tenderness in his eyes.

"Why do you tell me these things?" She looked perturbed. She turned and began to walk away. "I have to go. I've new slaves to tend to."

She was surprised he didn't follow, but felt his eyes on her as she moved down the path and headed in the direction of her

67

home. She disappeared into the crowded marketplace without looking back.

She tossed her head, lifting her chin. So what if he thought he knew more than she did. What did it matter? There was no more reasoning between what he believed, than what she knew to be true. He had no proof, no more than she did.

The only thing that puzzled her was that he seemed so sure. She *wanted* to believe in her gods and what they did for her, the way he believed in his. He seemed to have no reservations about anything.

***

Chapter 9

Chaya smoothed out the orange-red silken fabric beneath her slender fingers. "This will do perfectly." She speculated, staring at the cloth in her hand. "It'll take the guest's breath away when they see her in it."

Tasia nodded, as she sat in the back section of Kalista's room. "Jewels won't be necessary with that color of tunic and her fiery hair. I can work wonders with those thick waves. She has no clue what a beauty she is." She fingered a pearl hairpiece from the box of precious stones. "It'll be the only adornment she'll need."

Chaya stood. "I need to bring this to the sewing room and fashion a pattern for it. I've an idea and will be back later."

Tasia set the hairpiece aside. "I'll clean up and get fresh water and food for her stand."

After Chaya left, Tasia couldn't help pulling jewels from the box and lifting them to her olive skin, wondering what it would be like to own such an assortment. Each of the pieces was delicately worked, exquisite in design. She wondered at the lack of diligence on the part of the staff to store them safely, and yet with so many riches, Kalista's jewels were most likely not as costly as the others.

She lifted the lid over the container and slid it back onto the shelf on the bed stand, noticing a small drawer she'd not seen before. Curious in nature, she opened it, pulling out letters written in Greek and a small wooden box. Not able to read the writing on the parchment, because she'd never been taught, she stuffed them back into the drawer.

Instead, her interest was in the box and what it contained. She pried the lid off, marveling at the pearl earrings inside, cut to perfection, smooth to the touch.

She wondered why the jewels were stored separately, hidden away in the chest as if to keep others from discovering them.

***

When Kalista came into the room and saw Tasia holding her mother's earrings, her hand immediately reigned down upon the slave, slapping her on the ear.

"Give them to me, you thief! Now!" She growled out her words. She opened Tasia's palm. What could have ever possessed the slave to go through her things?

Kalista held up her hand to strike Tasia again. But, she stopped when she noticed the young woman bowed in submission.

The jewels were her mothers! No one had the right to touch them!

Tasia's lashes fanned out on her cheeks. She peered at Kalista from beneath, a wounded expression in her eyes. She held the box out dutifully. "I meant no harm. I was curious. Please. I was going to put them back." She cupped her hand to her ear as if to quell the stinging.

Kalista grabbed the box, examining the pearls, placing them back inside the drawer. "Do you want to be dismissed, you imbecile? They're my personal possessions, and you've no right to go through them!"

The slave trembled. "Nona showed us your jewels, and I was deciding which ones you might wear, when I discovered the box. I've never stolen anything, I swear. And I promise, I'll never touch them again."

Kalista couldn't keep her eyes from Tasia who was cupping her ear. A picture of Domnica came into her mind, and she cringed inwardly. Was she no better than her fiendish stepmother?

Yet, she had good reason to slap the slave, didn't she? Maybe? But, maybe not.

Suddenly, she wished she'd listened first. She regretted how harsh she'd been and knelt down beside Tasia. "I've never done that before. But, those earrings are important to me. They're all I have."

Tasia lowered her head. "I won't do it again, ever."

Kalista sighed. "Please don't, or show them to anyone." She never wanted Domnica to find out about them. The thought of it made her cringe with fear. She could only imagine what her stepmother would do to the jewels, if she ever knew they belonged to Gabriella.

Tasia nodded, rubbing the side of her face. "I won't. I swear."

Kalista frowned. "They were a gift from my real mother. Domnica would smash them to pieces, if she knew I had them."

70

Kalista's Hope

Tasia reached out and took Kalista's hand in her own. "Your mother died, too?"

Kalista pulled back. There was a troubled expression on her face. "When I was born. But, I don't remember it, or her for that matter."

A raw hurt suddenly welled up inside her. She got up to leave. She didn't want to discuss something so significant in her life with this young woman.

"But, *she* knew you. And you were surely a gift before she died." Tasia spoke quietly.

"No." Kalista stopped and lowered her head. She suddenly felt as if she might be sick. "I need to get out of here."

"But, surely. Your mother must have seen a tiny infant as a gift? I think she would've adored you. You were kind to take me in."

Kalista shook her head. "It wasn't like that. I told you." She thought of the tombstone and the words on it. She was given life at the expense of her mother. She was the cause of so much grief. There was nothing anyone could do to take that away. She would always carry that pain inside of her.

"But, you were a baby." Tasia insisted, her eyes serious. "You'd no control over any of it. No one could help such a thing."

Tasia reached out and stroked her arm, smoothing back her hair.

Kalista closed her eyes. She wanted to run from this, but couldn't put to rest what Gaius told her and instead sunk down onto the rug beside Tasia. Maybe it would be good for Tasia to know the things she dealt with inside. "I was the cause of so much pain, regardless of whether I was a baby or not."

"Can I help?" Tasia took her hand. "Everyone needs someone who cares for them."

Kalista shook her head. "Not everyone."

But, droplets without warning began to slide over her cheeks, and she had no idea where they'd come from. They were in traces at first, and then in splashes. They came steady and strong.

Emotions hidden below the surface didn't prepare her for what was bubbling to the surface. She stiffened. This wasn't like her.

She grabbed lengths of her hair to sop the tears dropping on her face. Rawness tore at her insides, and she curled up in a

71

heap on the floor next to Tasia's straw mattress, holding the edge of it. She would allow herself this one cry.

Tasia put her hand on Kalista's shoulder, cooing to her ever so softly. "It's all right. Everyone needs to let go, sometime."

Kalista was sure the shadow on the sundial ran its course ten times over before she finally felt the last of the drops falling onto her cheeks. Her eyes were swollen and sore, and her face was raw and red. It wasn't like her to share her emotions with another person, and she felt drained and out of control, like she'd been let out of a cage after years of confinement and didn't know what to do.

She looked up, and a frown drew across her brow. She quickly wiped her eyes and looked away, realizing she'd lost track of all time. Tasia was still beside her, a concerned look on her face.

"Miss?" she inquired. "Will you be all right?"

Kalista pushed her hair out of her face. She shrugged, trying to appear as if nothing happened. "Please," she said quietly. "Don't tell anyone? You understand?"

Tasia lay down upon her pallet and shook her head, her eyes fixed on the frescos adorning the wall. She nodded.

"Good, there's no reason for it." Kalista breathed a sigh of relief.

Exhausted, she went back to her own bed, pulling a woolen wrap tightly around her, sinking her head down onto her pillow. She wondered where all these outpourings of emotion were coming from lately. She hated the loss of control she felt over herself and her life. She wished she'd never spoken to Gaius.

***

When Tasia came out the next morning to wake her, her silent demeanor and constrained lips gave indication to Kalista as to the character of her new servant, one who was not willing to betray her. Kalista shuddered a sigh, realizing she might be able to trust the girl to work for her good. She felt bad for slapping her and vowed it would never happen again.

***

Chaya spread the orange-red silk out in front of her, encircled by the other women around her in the small room. She leaned closer to a small child sitting next to her and pointed to the embroidery she was teaching the little girl. "This is a square. If

Kalista's Hope

you put gold stitching around it, it will bring out the green shades behind it." She patted the little child's head.

The curly, blonde-headed girl looked up, smiling. "It's pretty, Chaya."

Nona nodded. "You've a way with style and design. Are you thinking to buy your freedom with your talent?"

Chaya smiled. "Maybe. But mostly, to get out of here to find someone." Her solemn eyes glowed with the thought. She lifted her needle to the orange fabric and began to stitch.

It was not as if she resented being in the Neo household. She was treated well in the home and given a position of authority over other servants who'd been there longer than she was.

And yet, there was a longing inside her she couldn't deny. She couldn't help thinking of Atticus, or why her sisters did what they did.

She wondered what had become of the man she'd met soon before being sold into slavery. She recalled the time they were together only months before.

Their first meeting was on a summer day that drove heat into the valley where she lived. She was on the hillside near her home gathering grapes from a vineyard.

When she turned around to trade baskets with an empty one on the ground, Atticus was coming up the hill. She'd taken a step back at first, but then smiled.

His lopsided grin and clear blue eyes gave her indication that she had nothing to fear and that she could trust him.

"Here." He took the full basket from her. "I'll carry it back when you're ready, if you'd like."

She eyed him curiously, noticing the lute that hung from his shoulder by a leather cord. She wondered if he could sing, as she loved music, too.

She shook her head gratefully, then turned back to her work, filling the second basket.

"What's your name?"

She hesitated, wondering at his forwardness.

"You can tell me. I live just outside of town. We're practically neighbors."

She smiled. "It's Chaya."

"And I'm, Atticus." His teeth sparkled in straight rows.

She admired the kindness he showed to her, and the honesty in his expression.

73

Kara S. McKenzie

He waited for her to finish her work, asking her questions, until he knew more about her than most of her family did. When all the grapes filled the buckets, she sat down on the ground admiring the lush fields and wildflowers around them.

He took the lute from his shoulder and began to play. Deep, rich sounds belied any doubts she might've had that he could sing. His song rose over the hillside. She was lost in the gentle sway of his music.

When he was done and put the lute away. He told her more about himself. She learned he was a carpenter in the next town and lived there for the better part of his life and was on his way home this evening. "When I saw you on the hillside, something tugged at my heart. I knew I had to meet you." Unexpectedly, he reached out and took her hand, and she didn't resist. "I'll walk back with you."

She nodded.

He carried both baskets back for her. When they reached the house, he told her that he wanted to see her again.

She felt the blush on her face, and smiled at his suggestion.

Over the next months, Atticus came often, and their friendship grew along with their love for each other.

Chaya never forgot the day he made his intentions clear. He told her he would come back to visit her father to ask for her hand in marriage the next day. When he left, he turned once to lift his hand and wave. Her heart overflowed with love for him. She didn't know that things would change very quickly, and he'd not see her when he returned.

The next day, she landed on a caravan headed for Rome, sold by one of her sisters. Her youngest sister, steeped in jealousy, had devised a way to try and take center place in her parent's lives. Chaya never heard from Atticus again, but refused to forget the months she spent in his company and how much she'd grown to care for him.

"Chaya?" Nona questioned her.

She lifted her head.

"You've only until tomorrow to finish the dress."

Chaya lifted the needle to the fabric, pushing her thoughts aside. Nona was right. If she wanted to find a way out of this mess, she needed to work hard and prove she was worthy of more than the life of a slave.

***

74

Kalista's Hope

Atticus slammed the nail into the piece of wood, forgetting his task. Lately, he couldn't keep his mind on his work. He didn't buy the story Chaya's sister fed to their father. He was with Chaya that evening and had taken her back to the house safely. There was no reason for her to go back out to get more baskets. She had finished her work that night.

Something wasn't right. A tunic bloodied, with no scratches upon it, and no body? They would have found her if she was at the orchard. None of it made sense. And he didn't trust her youngest sister. He'd speak to travelers on the road and find out what he could. He wouldn't give up searching, until he knew the truth.

***

Chapter 10

Domnica smiled. She leaned against a column supporting the roof surrounding the garden, seemingly pleased with her gown of dark blue silk that hugged her body, revealing her curves.

Kalista was sure her stepmother purposely instructed her seamstresses to create her stolas as such to give her this desired effect.

She eyed Domnica suspiciously. Her stepmother was obviously up to something, by the expression on her face. Something stuck in the pit of Kalista's stomach as she watched her.

"We've decided you'll be wed." Domnica's dark eyes sparkled with the news. "It's for the best for all of us concerned."

Kalista crossed her arms in front of her. "Father wouldn't do this." She made a face.

"But, he already has. Camila saw you talking to a man at the Gates of Janus. And you've been running with that boy Justus to all sorts of public places in that filthy attire, making a mockery of your father's good name. I told him he needed to do something about it, and we both agreed that you'll marry within the year."

The news cut Kalista to the quick. She glowered at Domnica. "You're lying!" She stomped over to where her stepmother stood, her sandals clapping hard against the marble tiles.

Domnica sneered. "Oh, but it's true. And you'll finally stop this foolishness. The man's already been chosen for you, and there's nothing you can do about it."

Camila was watching from a small wooden bench in the garden next to a huge fountain. She had a wry smile on her face. "Serves her right she ends up with a man who'll teach her how to behave. He doesn't seem to mind what he's getting."

Kalista cheeks flamed. "*She* knows who it is, before I do?" The thought of this sent fire running through her veins. She wanted to choke the sense into both of them.

Domnica grinned maliciously. "He'll be a suitable match for you, Kalista. I can't imagine why your ridiculous looks and boyish personality don't deter him." She brushed at the folds of her gown, as if some imaginary piece of lint were on it.

Kalista's Hope

Kalista's eyes narrowed. "I don't care about him, or any of them you'd choose." But, the fact that Domnica was able to involve her father in this, made her stomach churn inside. The palms of her hand began to sweat, and she wiped them on her tunic.

"Maybe he's not able to get anyone else. He *is* old." Camila laughed again. She tipped her head back, the ringlets from the piles of hair on her head bouncing as she spoke. She pushed back a ribbon that pulled free from the stack and secured it beneath a coiled braid.

Kalista balled her fist. Her eyes smoldered as she looked at both of them. "Enough! I've had it with the both of you!" She wondered who the man was. She didn't like the sounds of him and couldn't imagine the choice Domnica would have made. The thought of it made her boil inside.

"Well." Domnica sneered at her. "It's mutual then! I've had enough of you, too."

She motioned to the two slaves standing next to her to come forward. "Take her to her chambers, and have her cleaned up. From now on her hair will be carefully arranged, and she'll be wearing suitable clothes for her status."

And then she turned, eying Kalista as if she were the entertainment. "And tell them to have her ready for the dinner party, tomorrow." A malicious curve emerged on her lips. "Barbatus Porcius will be there, and he'll wish to see what he's getting."

Kalista stormed over to her, stomping her sandals against the stone tiles beneath her. "Barbatus? Of all the no good men you could have picked." An explosive rage steamed inside her at this latest venomous deed. It wasn't going to happen, if she'd have anything to say about it.

Domnica's eyes sparkled, and she seemed pleased by Kalista's reaction to her news. "He has connections, and is in the political field. You'll be well set. I encouraged your father in the decision, and he agreed." She smiled, with something akin to poison in her eyes.

Kalista bristled. "I should've known you'd have something to do with it." She tossed her head defiantly and crossed her arms. "And if you think I'll have anything to do with any detestable dinner party he'll be at, you're wrong. I want nothing to do with that man."

77

Kara S. McKenzie

"Ah, but your father told me you'd go. You can defy me, but you won't defy him." She had a smug expression on her face.

Kalista looked at Domnica through narrowed slits. Her stepmother would rue the day she ever got her father involved in any of this. She boiled inside and felt a flame growing inside her, yet said nothing.

Domnica took a seat on one of the lounging chairs and settled herself against a cushion. She lifted her hand to the servants next to her and snapped her fingers, smiling. "You know what to do with her."

Kalista could hear her stepmother's laughter behind her, as two of the male slaves took her by the arms and led her out of the room.

Outside the door, Kalista angrily shook them off. "I know my way to my chambers. You don't need to manhandle me like a prisoner in my own home."

Both men looked at each other and nervously eyed the door. "But miss..."

Kalista scowled, "She won't know. And if I were you, I'd worry more about my father, than her."

They let go of her, but walked behind, making sure she made it and locking the door behind her.

***

In her room, Kalista paced the floor, tapping her fingers against the side of her gown. Barbatus Porcius.

She fumed at her stepmother's words. She stalked over the tiles, her mouth drawn into a tight line, knowing she'd have the last say in this. Even her father had less control over her than he imagined. She'd rather be dead than marry that ridiculous man. She'd find a way to get back at all of them. For this, they would pay.

***

Kalista entered the room, the dinner party in full swing. Thick waves of reddish blonde hair flowed over her shoulders, tied back with a pearl comb. The orange-red tunic of silk Chaya fashioned for her, swirled out behind her as she walked. Every eye was upon her, as she paced across the mosaic tiles to her seat, her dark, cinnamon eyes fixed straight ahead.

A great hush fell over the room when she took a place on a wooden chair at the far end of her father's table. She gritted her teeth, as she leaned against the back of the chair. Her father had forced her to come the party, but she wasn't intending on staying.

Kalista's Hope

She wondered where that pig of a man was, whom they were threatening to marry her off to.

Camila's eyes sparkled. She straightened in her seat, gloating, and began primping tendrils of blonde hair that fell over her shoulder. She murmured something to a young girl with dark brown hair sitting beside her, and they both cackled with laughter.

Kalista narrowed her eyes at the both of them. They could laugh, but what Camila didn't know, was that she wasn't going to submit to anything Domnica and her father planned for her.

An elderly woman at another low table in the room leaned over and touched her husband's shoulder. "I thought her to be particularly handsome, yet now I think I was mistaken. She's lovely."

The man nodded. "Yes. Barbatus will be pleased."

Everyone in the room began to whisper like ripples from a fountain. Barbatus swiveled around to see what all the commotion was about, and his eyes gleamed when he spotted Kalista.

Kalista thought he looked like a greasy pig with his little eyes and thick fingers and chubby face. He sat there rubbing his hands together, staring at her with interest. His robe was carelessly draped across his hairy chest and the belt across his waist was sagging beneath his portly stomach. Not the type women were falling over themselves for.

She ignored the incessant hum around her, all the while contemplating how she'd escape the party at her earliest convenience.

Sweeping a strand of bright red hair over her shoulder, she sat upright, barely touching the food in front of her, seething inside.

How could her father even stoop so low as to try and marry her off to a rat as worthless as Barbatus? Somehow Domnica convinced him, the man would be beneficial to her.

Her father was at the end of the table, sitting next to the scoundrel.

Barbatus smoothed his slightly graying hair and lifted an egg off one of the platters. He put it to his mouth and began to suck on a portion of it, his eyes still fixed on Kalista while he ate.

Kalista was livid with anger at the thought of him. From what she knew, the greedy swine earned his riches dealing in some type of illegal trade. Justus said he was a frequent visitor at

79

Kara S. McKenzie

the brothels at night and spent large amounts of time in dog-eared shops her father wouldn't be caught dead in. No doubt he wished to bolster his public image by marrying her.

Kalista snorted, amused. If his plans ever came to pass, Barbatus would regret ever having set eyes on her. No man with any sense in his head would bind her to him without her willing consent. She'd surely make life miserable for anyone daring to try.

***

Dinner parties were something Gaius usually tried to avoid, as he considered them extravagant affairs, set up by influential people to flaunt their money in business deals with each other. He came at the request of his father, but wished to have no part in the games the people here played.

He turned to the source creating a buzz on the other side of the room.

His mouth drew open. "Huh…" He choked and swallowed when his eyes lit on the young woman poised on the chair at the end.

Kallie?

He was astonished by the transformation, unable to take his eyes from her. Her skin looked like creamy satin beneath the mass of neatly coiffed curls swept from her face with a pearl comb.

The orange-red gown with gold, satin ties crossing beneath her breasts, fanned out around her like a flame. Her face was free from dirt and grime, revealing a dusting of freckles over her nose and cheeks, and her large, luminous eyes could only be described as haunting. He likened her to a Greek statue or a caged bird trying to take flight.

It unnerved him to see other men eying her the way they were. Capable though he knew her to be, they could only ruin what little spark remained amidst the ashes of her brokenness.

***

As the evening wore on, Kalista barely touched the appetizers at her table, followed by the six-course meal and dessert. She purposely grasped meat on a tray with all five fingers, pleased at the gasps rising up around her.

Camila muttered words to Kalista under her breath. "Three fingers, you idiot!"

Kalista's Hope

Kalista practically burst in laughter for the first time of the night. Phooey on their etiquette! Barbatus knew nothing about the young woman he was getting involved with, the poor dupe.

She swiveled around and noticed Gaius for the first time that evening. He was sitting at a table on the other side of the room watching her. Her brow rose at the glow in his eyes and the half smile on his face. She tipped her head to the side, unsure whether she relished the idea of him being present at the meal, or bothered by it.

She wondered if she might find a time to speak with him when the meal was finished. The guests were leaving to another room for their entertainment soon. She'd been crafting a plan in regards to her situation. It might be a good time to let him in on it.

Soft melodies of lutes sounded from the adjoining room as other guests rose from their seats, making their way into the garden. In the flood of brightly colored togas and stolas, they made their way into the open room in the center of the home.

Kalista excused herself from her seat and took hold of her dress, lifting the edge, careful not to trip, motioning to Gaius with her eyes to follow her into the adjacent room. She watched to see if he understood and would follow her.

He took the cue and lit by her side as they entered the Peristylium, the indoor garden room full of fragrant lilies and rosebushes, placed strategically around statues and furniture.

A crowd gathered near a man, who stood up to read.

Kalista found her way to some artwork, which was hanging on walls encircling the garden under the overhanging roofs. She pretended to admire a painting hanging from one of them, while waiting for Gaius to catch up with her.

Gaius edged up behind her, leaning over her shoulder observing the colors and lines in the work. "You wanted to speak with me? After last time, I'm surprised." His voice was a whisper. There was a hint of humor in it.

Kalista turned. "Why not?" And then she tugged on his shirt, speaking in a half desperate tone. "I need you to do something, Gaius."

He laughed, his blue eyes suddenly sparkling. "Need? I'm not sure whether to believe that. You seem to do rather well on your own."

She ignored him and gently pushed him away. "Please. I don't know what to do. Can we talk outside the house by the walk? I'll tell them I've a headache and find my way to the front of the house. Can you wait for me there?"

In his face was something akin to amusement. "I'll see what I can do." He backed up to let her go past and waited there a moment, as in deep admiration of the painting.

Kalista managed to slip away from the group with little notice and went to one of the side doors where she'd directed him. The night was warm and the sky clear, a large moon lighting the path. Kalista lifted her gown to keep it clean so there'd be no evidence of her departure from the great house.

She rounded a tall statue of two men engaged in battle and jumped when she ran almost directly into Gaius.

"You could've let me know you were here." She pushed him backward, accusatory.

He stepped away from her, a smile forming on his face. "I thought it was supposed to be a discreet meeting."

She made a sound and pulled him behind the statue, putting her fingers to her lips. "It is, and if you're not quiet, you'll give us away. I'm supposed to be in my room resting." Her eyes scanned the grounds, making sure they weren't followed.

He reached out and put his hand on her arm. "All right. I see you're upset. So, what's your problem? And why did we have to come out here to talk?"

Kalista looked annoyed. "You know Barbatus Porcius? That man who was sitting with my father tonight?"

Gaius suddenly seemed interested. "Yes. So what does he have to do with it, a business deal with your father? Or something like that?"

"Well, yes, something like that." And then she looked at the ground, a soft blush rising in her cheeks. For some reason, she found it difficult to tell Gaius what she knew.

He reached out and tugged on a length of her hair. "It can't be as bad as all that, can it?" He smiled. "What's happened?"

She bit her lip, not quite knowing how to tell him.

"Kallie?" There were questions in his eyes. "What is it? What does Barbatus have to do with what you have to tell me?"

Her throat was dry, and she choked on her words. "My father's going to give me to him in marriage."

A lump formed in Gaius' throat. He looked troubled by her news. "Barbatus?"

82

Kalista's Hope

She lifted her head, her eyes hard. "My stepmother recommended it, and my father, well…with him it's pay back for what I did to my mother. I'm sure."

When she saw the questions form in Gaius' eyes, she explained it to him. "She died in childbirth, after she had me."

Gaius' eyes gentled. "Kallie, I'm sorry. Your father shouldn't blame you for that."

"Only he does…yet, I can't think of that now." Kalista stated it matter-of-factly.

She steeled herself, pulling the pearl comb from her hair and gnawing on the edge of it.

She looked away from Gaius, who was staring at her, a somber expression on his face. Her eyes drew into a frown. "I don't quite know how to say this, but I'm thinking you might be able to help me out of the mess I'm in."

"But, how?" Gaius was clearly puzzled. "What can I do? I'll try if I can?"

She pulled on the teeth of the comb, fiddling with it.

Gaius reached out and held her hands still. He was suddenly serious. "Stop, and tell me what you want, Kallie."

Kalista hesitated, her cheeks beginning to burn. She shifted uncomfortably. "I thought that I might marry you." She felt as if she died a hundred deaths saying it, but knew it was her only hope in finding a way out of her marriage to Barbatus.

She let out a breath, and then looked up at him. "I know I'm not much, but my father, he does have a fortune."

"Marry?" Gaius let out a low whistle. He shook his head, as if trying to make sense of what she just told him.

"Well, yes. Like I said, my father…he's a Roman consul. You'd benefit from such an arrangement." She knit her brows together. Most people would kill for such a position offered to them. Yet, why did she think that it might be different with Gaius?

Gaius looked annoyed. "I don't need your father's money, Kallie. And it's not why I'd marry anyone." He eyed her with uncertainty.

She tugged at her hair, twisting it around her finger. "But, I've little else to offer. It's why Barbatus wants this deal to go through, and why anyone else would. It's my money and things that matter to them."

He looked at her with compassion. "But, that's not true. You've a whole lot to offer, only I don't think you know it."

83

Kara S. McKenzie

She tipped her head to the side, eying him warily. "But, *you* wouldn't want anything I had." She suddenly felt broken inside. She couldn't even convince Gaius, with all the wealth and prestige she could give him.

"It isn't that I wouldn't want *you*." He pulled at the collar on his tunic and looked uncomfortable, as his eyes lingered on a length of auburn hair that had fallen over her shoulder. "But, I can't."

She sat down at the base of the statue, pushing the strand behind her. Didn't he know what her father's riches could do for him? Did he understand the power he'd have, if he married her? "But, why? I don't understand."

Gaius took a place next to her, taking her hand in his. "In the Christian writings, there are passages that warn of marriage to an unbeliever, that it's not what God intends." He had a concerned look in his eye and something akin to disappointment was also present. "It's not easy for me to reject your proposal, but I must."

She lifted her chin and pulled her hand away. "You're basing your decision on what those teachings say?" She couldn't believe he'd turn her down because of his beliefs. "Because of your religion?" She clenched her hands into fists and held them to her sides. How he could do such a foolish thing?

She could feel the bitterness of the past mushrooming inside her, and she practically choked on the anger that threatened to spill out of her. She turned away.

"Kallie. I'm sorry." There was genuine regret in his voice when he said it. "My life isn't my own, and I can't make these choices for myself. You don't understand what you're asking of me."

She could tell he meant what he said, but didn't understand it, his life not his own? Whose was it, then? The whole idea was absurd.

Her look was one of unbelief, and she put her hand to her mouth, holding back laughter. "This is ridiculous. I never heard anything like this. Of all the weak-willed, silly beliefs I've seen, this one takes the emperor's crown."

He shrugged. He eyed her resolutely, as if the harsh words had little effect on him. "I won't argue for my religion, or against it. You can say what you want. But, if it's not God's will for a believer to marry someone with different views, I won't do it."

Kalista's Hope

She let out an annoyed sound and slanted her eyes at him. "Oh, I see. So, you find me lacking." He didn't think she was good enough for him. That was it.

Gaius shook his head. "No. Not at all." He pointed to a statue of two oxen pulling a wagon. "When the team is pulling the same direction, it's a good match, you see?"

She bristled. "No. You don't make sense."

"Callie. If in marriage, I'm following God and his will, and you're pulling in a different direction, then time spent together would be like unevenly yoked oxen. Have you ever seen a field hand trying to work with such a pair?"

She pursed her lips. "Yes, but…no, I mean, surely you're not likening us to this?"

"I want to help you, Kallie, but my faith in God isn't something I take lightly. When there's something written in his Word that's clear to me, I follow it. I don't want to turn from what God says, no matter how much I might want to."

"Hah!" She shook her head, incredulously. "I don't care what you do. I didn't really think you'd agree anyway."

"Kallie, don't be like this." Gaius sighed and tried to grab her hand.

She quickly got up and waved him away. "No! Don't worry about it. I'll figure something else out. I don't need you."

He stood behind her. "You do understand, don't you?"

She lifted her shoulders and straightened her back, her eyes like daggers. "I always thought the Christian's teachings absurd, but this is almost laughable. Your foolish beliefs will ruin both our lives. You could've had so much wealth and prestige, more than you'd ever come into on your own. And you let it all go on some ludicrous commitment to a God you can't even see."

Her voice lowered to a whisper. "If I were Camila, you might see things differently. It's not difficult for her to get the men she wants."

She looked toward the house. This very instant, Camila was probably, surrounded by young suitors, while she flicked her silky, honey-blonde hair behind her, giggling at everything they said. Well, appearances didn't mean everything…or did it? She couldn't help it she was born with this untamable hair and upturned nose and had been called small and slight.

Gaius expression was serious. "Kallie, you're very pretty, do you understand? It's why Barbatus wants you."

Kara S. McKenzie

She laughed. "Yeah, then why aren't other young men falling over themselves in pursuit of me, I'd like to know?" Tears began to sprout to her eyes, but she held them back.

He reached out and gently pushed a strand of her hair back from her face. "Because you haven't given them a chance. And none of them have been able to see through the grime and dirt and messed up hair, until now."

He smiled. "Except for me. I knew you were a beauty from the first day I met you. And I also know you have a good heart beneath the pretense of the scowl you wear on your face."

She looked surprised. "That's hard to believe." She was puzzled by the way he was staring at her.

"But, it's more than that." He suddenly looked frustrated. "I think you're very beautiful."

She felt heat rising in her face, complimented by what he said, but had a hard time believing him, even though he looked sincere. She eyed him with uncertainty. "But, what about spending time in my company? You like this?"

"Have I ever declined a walk with you?"

She didn't answer at first and then shook her head. "No."

She let out an agitated breath. "Yet, your God keeps us from each other, when it could be good."

He took a step back from her and let out a breath. "But, it wouldn't, for either you or I. We've separate beliefs and wouldn't understand each other. I'm hoping someday you'll see my God is good, and you'll turn to him."

"So, until then, you'll turn your back on me?" Her eyes were dark and stormy. She pursed her lips.

He didn't answer. There was a painful look in his eyes.

She sniffed. "As I said, it's a ridiculous belief you hold to, and I want none of it. I'll find my own means to rid myself of Barbatus. I'll see to that. I don't need you to help me find a way out of it."

Gaius studied her quietly, his look affectionate. And then he smiled. "I don't doubt it, Kallie." He opened his mouth to speak again, but before he could answer, she turned from him and started down the path.

"Kallie, please try to understand."

She kept walking, turning only once. "I don't want to understand you. And don't call me Kallie. I'm not special to you. Go back to your people and your silly prayers, and someday you'll realize how preposterous they are."

Kalista's Hope

***

Gaius stood on the grounds behind her, his head bowed and lips moving silently.

He willed himself not to go after her and prayed that he could wait for God's response and timing for something he had no right to consider on his own. He wanted what was best for Kallie and had to believe that God would protect her from Barbatus.

***

Chapter 11

Kalista knew Justus would help.

She scanned the street and spotted him standing just on the other side of his father's high-rise apartments. Perfect timing.

It was a relatively quiet day in the city, maybe because the sun had just risen and there were still few people on the streets. It might take an hour or two before the drunks of the previous night would rouse themselves to seek the gods. So, until then, she had the place to herself.

"Justus!" Kalista called out to him. The damp, cool morning air of the city swept over her, and she yanked her shawl tighter. The wooden apartments rose above them on all sides, while rows of windows faced them like eyes, watching and waiting.

She tipped her head to the god of the Northwest wind, Corus, hoping he'd lesson the morning chill because she took the time to acknowledge him. If not, the sun god would surely oblige.

Justus glanced up and waved from a distance, waiting for her, his thin legs awkward in their stance. "I thought you'd be at Janus at this time. I was on my way there!" He began walking toward her.

Kalista's eyes were drawn to his father's apartment directly above him. She noticed the teetering and swaying of it in the wind. It was precariously built and given to movement and sound, like so many places in the city. Justus had lived there for years.

"There's something I must ask you!" She shouted back to him, lifting her silk gown to keep from tripping, as she made her way down the street. "It couldn't wait!"

She stopped a second time, again noting the movement of the building. Something about the way it tilted and tottered was different today, unnatural.

Both of them turned to look up.

When a rumbling came from the top of the structure, Kalista's breath caught in her throat. "Justus?"

He stopped in his tracks, and his eyes grew large, seeing the ramshackle building suddenly start collapsing from the top.

He remained motionless, gaping at it, his mouth open.

Kalista's Hope

Kalista watched a chunk of the structure topple over the side. "Look out!" She shrieked wildly to him. "Run, Justus!"

As each successive floor began to burst apart, there was an intense roaring like a violent windstorm growing more powerful as it neared the bottom.

People from inside the lower floor raced out the door, their faces white, looking up all the while. They bolted out into the middle of the street trying to get as far from the building as they could.

Justus looked terrified. He turned back and screamed. "Father!" He tore off in the direction of the doorway and then realized it was too late and turned back again.

Kalista shrieked his name. "Justus!"

He dodged part of the roof that almost caved in on top of him and raced down the street to where Kalista stood. He was holding his head in his hands, looking behind him. "No!" He cried out, a strangled sound coming from his throat.

All eight stories came crashing down. There were muted screams coming from inside the building. A smashing of roughshod timber splintered into pieces, and plumes of dust and air rose around the outside of the structure.

People from adjacent buildings hurried out to watch in horror.

Justus sank to his knees and grabbed the top of his head in his hands. "Father!"

Kalista hurried and bent down next to him. She clasped her arms around his shoulders, eying the collapsed building reduced to rubble in the distance.

She couldn't believe what had just happened. She'd heard of such a thing before with these tall, wobbly structures, but never thought of it happening to anyone she knew. She shook her head. Justus' father had little chance of ever being found alive in the mess.

An eerie silence swept the streets like a melancholy flood. People stared at the debris, dumbfounded. The cobblestone streets seemed to be the only thing around the apartments left intact.

Justus pushed Kalista away and got up to survey the damage. He sprinted to the pile and began to dig, scraping away the dirt with his fingers and yanking pieces of timber wedged in the rubble. "He's in here. Maybe still alive." His voice was a whisper.

89

Kara S. McKenzie

Kalista was still unable to speak. Justus' father's apartment was on the top floor. Rarely, when these buildings collapsed, were there any survivors. Her heart went out to him, knowing what it was like to be without a parent. Now, Justus had lost his second.

Justus clawed at the debris, pulling pieces out and pushing aside large fragments of wood. He kept digging, until he realized he was only making a dent in the huge mound and his efforts were in vain. He got up from where he was and let out a groan, tears on his face.

Slaves from across the street moved in under the direction of a shop owner nearby. They began using tools to dig, looking for survivors. They were well-muscled men, shackled to their owner with chains. The irony of them working to free others, when their own lives were bound, was not lost on Kalista. There was so much in this world that didn't make any sense to her.

Moments later, someone screamed. "A man and a small child!"

Kalista pointed to the body being dragged out into the street. "Justus?"

He didn't move at first, and then he got up, recognizing the brown wool tunic his father was wearing earlier that day. "It's him."

He took quick steps to the spot. "Papa!" He leaned down, cradling the older man in his arms. He rocked back and forth and groaned, a pitiful sound. "Papa."

He looked lost and stared at Kalista, unblinking.

"I'm so sorry, Justus. He was a good man." Kalista couldn't help but shed tears. She couldn't have imagined what it might feel like for Justus, to see the accident firsthand. She'd never thought she'd ever watch her friend's father die in such a way.

Justus looked to where there was a statue of Fortuna, goddess of fate. A piece of lumber was balanced on her arm, leaning against her head. He quickly turned away, his eyes suddenly hard.

"Sir." One of the slaves came and stood next to him. "A wagon was sent to load the bodies on. When you're ready, I'll instruct them to take your father. His body must be tended to." He waited for Justus' response.

Justus blinked. He seemed unaware of the shock that had settled over him.

Kalista's Hope

"They have to take him." Kalista put her hand on his arm. "You have to tell them what to do."

He loosed his grip on his father and sounded as if he were choking. "I need to know where they'll be taking him."

The man sighed. "We'll see he's cared for in the proper way. And then we'll send word to you after the arrangements are made. Where will you be?"

Justice pointed down the street. "The house on the corner, my cousin's. Let them know, and they'll get word to me."

"All right."

Kalista took Justus' hand and lifted him to his feet, her arm around him. He went with her to a small shop across the street where they sat down on a bench and watched while others continued to dig in hopes of finding survivors.

She took his hand in hers and held it, unable to comprehend what had just happened. What was the purpose to living, when everything came to an end so suddenly? When would her time come, and what would happen to her? Would she be reduced to a load of rubble, to be carted away and hauled off as Justus' father had, or would some other tragedy strike without warning? Life was fragile and death came, whether a person was ready for it or not.

Her hands began to shake, and she held them as steady as she could by her side. She pushed a tear from her face and sat next to Justus silent, knowing what he needed now was not words, but a friend by his side.

They stayed there past noon and then into the evening hours.

Once dark was closing in, she finally spoke. "What will you do?"

Justus shook his head. "I don't know. I've nothing, only the books he left on the cart for me to take to Naples. He wanted me to open a shop there for him." He gripped his chest and groaned.

"Naples? Near Pompeii?"

"Yes, north of there."

There was silence again. Kalista shuddered. She didn't think this was the time to tell him what she'd come for, so didn't say anything.

She got up to leave. "Come, Justus, there's nothing more you can do. I need to help you find a place to stay for a time."

91

Kara S. McKenzie

Justus sighed, not moving. "No, I've father's books and the cart. I can't leave them. They're all I have. Like I said. My cousins live next door."

She was concerned. "But, what will you do? You can't stay with them long."

"Father said he wanted me to take the books. He said there was too much competition in Rome, and he gave me enough money to set up a shop."

She let out a breath, realizing maybe there was a duel purpose in her coming. Maybe it was the right time.

She put her hand on his shoulder. "Justus, I came to tell you something before all this happened. I understand the timing is poor, yet what I need to say might benefit us both in a time like this." She sucked in a breath.

His eyes were glassy and far away, yet he seemed interested.

She shrugged, resigned to what she had to say. "My father plans to marry me off...to Barbatus Porcius."

She nodded when he looked at her surprised.

He stammered, "You?"

"Yes, well...I'm not going to. I already made up my mind about it. No way will that greasy pig have what he wants...or Domnica for that matter."

His eyes widened. "But, you can't defy your father."

Her eyes narrowed, and she pursed her lips. "I have to, unless I want to suffer that ridiculous man as a husband. I actually came to you with a plan, but when you mentioned Naples, I thought I might be of help."

"Naples?" He let out a breath, still eying the refuse across the street with a tragic look.

Kalista nodded. "Yes. I'm sorry. I know you don't need to think about things right now, but I must tell you. Otherwise, it'll be too late." She scrunched the gown she wore with her fingers.

"Just say it."

Justus' eyes were weary, but Kalista could tell he was receptive to what she had to say.

She reached out a comforting hand. "After this happened, I had an idea. It wasn't why I came. But, maybe we can help each other. If you'd have me, it'd be my greatest wish to go to Naples with you."

"Naples? With me?"

92

Kalista's Hope

"Well, I was thinking Pompeii. It's where my mother's from. She'd surely have had relatives there." Her breath caught in her throat as she spoke.

On the outside, she was calm, but felt a jumble on the inside. Seeing the place where her mother was born, or meeting relatives of hers from the past, would be everything she'd ever longed for during her young life and would become a reality if Justus went along with this.

His face was still white. "But your father. He'd come after us. That could mean something very bad for me."

"Not the way I'm thinking; he won't." She patted his hand.

He eyed the slaves lifting his father onto a mat and went over to touch his arm before they put him onto their cart.

Kalista stood next to him. "I'm sorry, Justus." She put her hand on his shoulder.

He choked back a sob. "I can't believe he's gone." His body shook as he laid his head on the cart next to his father. "It still doesn't feel real to me."

The cart pulled away, and Justus watched as the horses clomped slowly down the cobblestone street and out of sight. He put his hand on his chest and sucked in a breath.

Kalista patted his arm. "I'll stay with you. We'll have each other."

He nodded. "I'm glad you came when you did. I don't know what I would've done, if I were alone here. My cousins are all at work."

Kalista smiled solemnly. "I'm so sorry for all of this, and for having to talk to you about plans in a time as this. But, I can't stay long."

"Yes well." He let out a breath. "I know my father would want me to find a way to make it without him. Please tell me what you're thinking."

She nodded, reticent to continue, but she knew she had to. "Well, I don't believe my father would make the effort to come after me…especially if he thought something happened to me."

Justus eyed her curiously. "Like what?"

She cautiously said the words. "Like died with your father." And then, she frowned. "Sorry, Justus. I know this must be painful for you."

His eyes were troubled looking, but he nodded to her. "It's all right. I have to know it, and we have to make decisions."

93

Kara S. McKenzie

Kalista had a determined look on her face. She'd finally be leaving them for good. She was sad for Justus, but wanted so much to leave Rome. "I know my father and Domnica would be glad to hear of this happening to me, as they've been wishing to rid themselves of me for years."

Justus nodded. "Sorry, but I think what you're saying is true. And this could work."

Kalista shrugged. Then, she patted his arm. "We could leave as soon as the funeral arrangements have been taken care of and your father's put to rest. I've money I've been saving for a trip there. As long as I don't take the slaves, there'd be no reason for them to come after us. You could send word to Nona of what happened and tell them no one found the body."

He tipped his head to her. "I'll do this, but must go to the funeral first, before we can leave. I'm sure I could stay with my cousins until then. Beginning of next week, we'll go. Where will you be?"

"A few days ago, with all this chaos over marrying, I hid my money and my mother's earrings near her grave, thinking it was time for me to leave. I'll get it and stay at an inn until the funerals over, and then I'll be outside the Gates of Janus on Dies Solis. If you bring your cart, we can leave from there."

He looked back at the remains lying strewn on the ground where his apartment stood just hours before and nodded. "All right, we'll go then."

Kalista squeezed his arm. "Is there anything else I can do?"

He shook his head. "Nothing. But, you mustn't stay here. If Domnica finds out you're still alive, we might never leave together."

"Yes, go to your cousin's, Justus. They'll help you."

"I will. They'll be back soon. The slaves will let me in."

She waved to him.

His shoulders slumped, as he took off in the direction of his relative's home.

***

Poppaea admired Nero's castle, her new home. Rooms were designed with lively frescos etched with gold on the ceilings and walls. There was a scent of rich, exotic foods. She stepped softly across polished tiled floors in her sandaled feet.

It was everything she sought to have for herself. And now, it was hers.

94

Kalista's Hope

Nero finally divorced that whimpering, ridiculous Octavia on the charge that the woman was barren. Now, her own name would be the one uttered daily from his lips, and she could easily manipulate his entire empire from where she stood.

She touched her rounded belly, one of the reasons for Nero's sudden marriage to her. The child would provide the heir he wished for.

The gods were in her favor, and Nero was clay in her hands.

***

Chapter 12

"We need to go, Kalista." Justus motioned to her from the wagon loaded with books.

She sighed, getting up from the base of Janus. How hard could it be for a god to answer her?

She went out the gates and strode over to Justus' cart, grabbing its side. She took one last look around and then caught a movement behind her.

"Where are you going?"

She jumped back. Gaius was making his way toward her.

Despite, the fact that he'd turned down her proposal, she couldn't help feeling a small spark in her that he might've had a change of heart. Her father's money was certainly something for any man to consider.

She sighed. But then, knowing how he felt about his beliefs and the type man he was, deep down, she knew he wasn't there to propose.

She tried to give him an offhand look, and yet she couldn't help wondering at what he was going to say.

He smiled confidently, pushing back his thick blonde hair, his dark blue eyes assessing her in his usual gentle manner.

If he could only see how ridiculous his religion was, then they might have had a chance.

She tilted her head upward, staring down her nose at him. "Justus and I are on our way to Pompeii."

His eyes were on the wagon and Justus, and then resting on her. He moved closer. "Pompeii?"

She could feel the nearness of him. She moved away from him, closer to the wagon.

"So, you're leaving now?"

She nodded. "And not coming back."

He just stared at her, as if he were disheartened by the news, but didn't say anything.

Her lips drew into a pout. She assumed he wasn't there to propose to her, as he would have tried to stop her by now. It bothered her that he'd choose his religion over her.

She lifted her chin, turning away, hoping the admission she was about to make, would wound him in some way, regardless of the fact that it wasn't true.

Kalista's Hope

"And we're married, too."

She thought she might've seen a flash of disappointment in his eyes for the briefest of seconds, but couldn't be sure. But, what did he care? He had his chance. He should've said yes when she asked him.

Justus was on the cart. He turned away from Gaius, a strange look in his eyes.

"Justus? Tell him that we were married." She prodded him to look back at them.

The younger man gave her a perturbed look. "Kalista…"

Kalista put her hands on her hips, defiantly. "It's true. Isn't it, Justus?" She hoped this one time Justus would go along with her. Gaius deserved to be spited for saying no to her.

Justus' eyes shifted to the front of the cart again. "Well…I…"

"Justus!" Kalista practically stomped the ground with her sandaled foot. Why couldn't he tell a lie for her, just this once?

He was clearly uncomfortable, fidgeting with the reins in his hands. "It's true that we are."

Kalista looked up at Gaius, lifting her chin higher. "See. I told you." She tried to appear triumphant.

Gaius took hold of her. He shook his head. "I don't believe it. He's lying for you." And then he smiled, a spark lighting his eyes.

She crossed her arms. "But, why would you think this?"

Gaius reached out, taking her hand. "I have my reasons." She couldn't miss the forever grin that seemed permanently sculptured to his face.

She wished he'd back off.

His eyes were on hers. He leaned down close to her ear and whispered. "I think you know I care for you. And I think God has other plans."

He was a little too close for her comfort. A flame lit in her cheek, but she acted as if nothing he said mattered. "That's ridiculous." She flipped her hair behind her and out of his reach. Her brow moved up a notch.

"Is it?" He grinned and winked at her.

She lifted her head, eying him with a pretended air of determination. "Gaius, you're going to make us late. We have to go now."

She pulled herself onto the seat of the wagon and sat down next to Justus and looked back at him one more time. "You had your chance and didn't want me. I think you made that clear." She turned facing the road.

Gaius laid his hand over hers. "But, you're wrong, Kallie. If things were different, I know I'd be taking you to Pompeii right now, instead of Justus. You *are* special to me."

His touch sent sparks of electricity through her. She wanted to leave, before she changed her mind. She pulled her hand back. "We've no time for this now. Justus and I have to get out of here. We're late already."

He sighed, and then spoke quietly. "I suppose."

He looked puzzled a moment and eyed her curiously. "And yet, maybe God brought us together for different reasons." He looked quietly resigned to this, a saddened expression settling in.

A crease line suddenly drew over her forehead, as if she'd just thought of something else she needed to tell him. "Gaius, please, don't tell any of this to my family. There are things they don't know about."

He nodded and stood back from the wagon.

"No, promise me." She was pleading. He couldn't tell anyone about the plans. It would ruin everything.

"I promise." His eyes never left her face.

Kalista turned to Justus. "Come, we have to leave." She couldn't bear to look at Gaius again.

Justus eyed her curiously. "Are you sure?" He looked back at Gaius, whose expression was solemn.

"Yes, please."

He shrugged his shoulders, realizing he'd get no other answer. "Ha!" He snapped the reigns.

Kalista felt the rocking motion of the cart and held the side of it with her hand, refusing to look back. She knew Gaius was watching from behind. Something inside her kept her from taking one last glance. She pushed away the gnawing feeling in her heart.

***

Gaius' eyes were trained on the cart heading to the main gate. He ignored the chill of the morning, keeping a careful eye on Kalista, straight-backed, her auburn hair spilling out over her shoulders. Was it a mistake to let her go?

He prayed to God that she would give him a signal. He'd surely go to her if she did.

Kalista's Hope

The cart stopped at the gate while Kalista and Justus spoke with the guard there, then moved out the massive, cold stone arches, beyond Gaius' sight.

She was on her way to Pompeii. He wondered if he'd ever see her again.

***

"Get Nona! I need to see her now!" Domnica glowered, directing a dead stare to one of the servants. "And bring that deviant slave girl Kalista purchased at the market. We need to get to the bottom of this." She pushed past one of the servants, her layered jeweled stola, swinging wildly behind her.

Domnica and Terentius waited in the triclinium, a small, square room with no windows. The walls were lined with low, flat cushioned benches and decorated with colorful paintings. There were four, small ornately carved stands for eating, strategically placed for drinks and food.

Terentius and Domnica sat upright on the benches rather than lounging, as they were accustomed to, while three slaves in rough tunics waved large fans over their heads. The room was unusually hot for the time of year, and tensions roiled between the two of them.

"Where could she be?" Terentius frowned. "Do you know how long she's been gone?"

"I haven't seen her for a couple days, but assumed she was staying in her room." Clearly agitated, Domnica tapped her fingers on the side of the bench. "We have wedding plans to take care of."

They both looked up when Nona came shuffling into the room with her head down. Tasia was at her side. "You called, mistress?"

Domnica stood up, towering above the woman, her foot tapping against the tiled floor. "Where is she? Why wasn't I informed of her disappearance?"

Nona's hands shook, and she folded them together to still the trembling. Her voice was a whisper. "I only got word just now from Justus' slave and was on my way to tell you."

"Tell us what?" Terentius scowled, "Out with it. Where'd she go?"

Nona whimpered. "Nowhere. They said she was in the collapse when the apartments fell. They found Justus' father dead, but there was no sign of her. They think she died in it, too,

99

and is somewhere in the ruins. Justus said she was there.
They've been looking for her for days."

Tasia slipped behind Nona and let out a wounded sound.

Domnica's eyebrow rose, and her face reddened. "Dead?
She can't be."

"It's what they told me."

Terentius stood up, his mouth a grim line. He suddenly
looked sick, as if the news had a grave effect on him, and his face
turned an ashen gray. He didn't say anything, but just stared
woodenly.

"What's going on?"

Everyone turned, when Camila came into the room,
sidling up to her mother.

Domnica repeated the news. "Justus' slave said his
father's apartment collapsed on Kalista, and they didn't find a
body."

Camila looked shocked. "What?"

Domnica nodded.

A rueful frown formed quickly on Camila's face. "It's too
bad." She eyed the young slave girl standing behind Nona.

Terentius finally spoke. "We have to send someone there
to see if we can find her body."

Dominica shrugged. "If they do, then you can give her a
proper burial." She laid a hand on his shoulder and cupped his
drawn face in her hands. "Don't you think this might be best, for
her and us?"

His face turned pale. "What have I done?" His voice
lowered to a whisper.

"Darling, you've done nothing. The girl's always taken
risks."

What she said was true, but Terentius thought it seemed
heartless to say it in that moment.

"Come, I'll have the slaves bring you some wine to settle
your thoughts. As for Kalista, you'll just have to try to forget the
whole matter."

Terentius suddenly looked very tired. the shadows
beneath his eyes darkened. He sat back down, placing his head in
his hands.

Domnica ordered one of the slaves standing next to them
to bring wine and glasses. She gently pressured her husband into
a reclining position on the padded benches and lay down beside

100

Kalista's Hope

him. "You'll be all right. Things will be better over time. You'll see."

Camila took hold of Tasia's arm, and pulled her out from behind Nona. "Kalista's not here anymore. Can I have her slaves?"

The side of Domnica's mouth twitched, and she seemed taken back for a moment, then she nodded. "I don't see why not?" She eyed the slave's dark hair pulled back loosely and spangles on her wrist. "Although, she seems a bit outlandish if you ask me."

Nona squeaked, "Can she stay in the same quarters? Your other slaves already fill all the beds in the rooms where you house them. She'd be less of a bother to you this way."

Camila nodded. "As long as she comes to my room before I get up, I don't care where she sleeps. But, she'd better not be late. I want her at my bedside in the morning to fix my hair and help me with my clothes."

Tasia bowed. "I'll come Miss, and do my best."

Camila's eyes narrowed. "You better."

Tasia bowed again, fingering the beaded bracelet on her wrist.

Domnica hastened, "You can go now, Nona. And take the slave with you. She'll report to Camila tomorrow morning."

"Yes, Mistress." Nona bowed and left the room with Tasia.

***

Chapter 13

Traveling by cart was slow. The trip took less than a week along with others in a caravan Justus and Kalista joined. Justus brought his father's slave, Zipor, a man who was trustworthy, for protection and strength if needed. Zipor stayed close to Kalista, as a reminder to others along the path that she wasn't to be disturbed.

Kalista was tired of riding for so long on the bumpy cart. She couldn't wait to finally find a place to stay for longer than a night. She wondered if she made a mistake leaving Gaius, but knew she had to put her thoughts behind her.

As they neared the city of Pompeii, she leaned forward, breathing in the salty air along the coastline. The breeze was mild and the climate temperate. There was a dark volcano rising up on the other side of the city. It gave the place a majestic look with its massive peak reaching up to the sky. A sliver of smoke trailed into the air above it. She watched the gray plume rise and disappear in the wind.

Sheep were quietly grazing on a slope next to the road. Kalista pointed to them.

Justus nodded. "The soil must be fertile because of the volcano. There are a lot of vineyards, too."

Kalista looked impressed. Pompeii was all that she had imagined it to be. She couldn't believe how far the city spread across the land, almost as large as Rome. It looked prosperous here, a place where they might do well. She couldn't wait to begin looking for her family members. Everything seemed to be going the way she'd dreamed for many years.

After speaking with the guard at the gate, Kalista and Justus were given entrance into the city.

"Where should we go first?" Kalista was curious.

Justus grinned. "I suppose through the main gate, and then figure it out after that."

Kalista smiled, and then sighed. She was in her mother's city finally, after all these years.

***

Pompeii was a bustling city inside strong, arched gates. People hurried along the paths carrying baskets of food and

Kalista's Hope

wares. Soldiers patrolled the streets, while children happily played, trailing their parents on small footpaths to their homes.

Like Rome, hundreds of gods were molded and shaped and set on the street corners within gated entrances. Kalista wanted to find out where the different gods in the city were located and get back into a routine of making her daily visits to them. She'd been uneasy, not being able to do this along the way on the trip. She hoped nothing would happen to either her or Justus because of it.

Justus eyed the buildings on both sides of them. "I guess we'll find a place to live, and I'll set up a bookshop. We'll look for a small apartment, with a couple rooms."

Kalista nodded. "We'll figure it out. I'm sure it won't be long before I find my relatives and you get situated with your business."

Then she laughed aloud. "I'm so glad to finally be here, and so happy you took me with you, so I might finally meet my relatives."

"Yes, it is good, and I hope you'll find them."

She clasped her hands together and looked over the city. "I hope so, too."

***

Chapter 14

Chaya and Tasia strolled down the cobblestone street arm in arm, chattering freely, with carefree expressions. To Camila, they looked more like free women than slaves. But, at least they were hers now, with Kalista gone for good. And yet, she wished she'd left one of them back at the estate.

Ariston wasn't much to look at, but he was there for protection. And three slaves might present a better picture of her father's wealth if she ran into anyone she knew.

"Oh, look!" Tasia bubbled with excitement. She pointed across the street to a dressmaker shop.

Camila waved a fan across her face and wrinkled her nose. "I can't imagine anything I'd want in a place as that." She wondered what Kalista was teaching these slaves, speaking so boldly. She should've been spending more time training them properly. Now, they were more difficult to deal with.

Tasia caught Chaya's eye and held back a grin, placing her hand to her mouth.

Camila was quick to catch the exchange, and her eyes became hard like stone. "You forget your place, Tasia. Remember, I own you." To think, the slaves had the audacity to be making faces in her presence.

Tasia apologized. "I only thought…"

Camila grabbed her by the arm, squeezing it with a force that hurt. "Don't. I do that." Her eyes glittered. She was getting tired of dealing with these worthless girls. She'd had enough of their antics. She looked back down the street.

She passed some men standing on the corner and ignored their stares. "Ugh, carpenters." They needed to move out of her way, rather than gawking at her like idiots. They should've realized the daughter of an aristocrat would have nothing to do with them.

She lifted her tunic and moved further down the street. Her eyes lit on a canopy bed in the path directly in front of her. Two slaves held poles that ran through rings attached to the sides. Inside was a girl peeking out from behind filmy curtains. Camila sighed when she realized who it was. Corvina. She wished she had spent more time on her hair.

Kalista's Hope

When the young woman under the canopy spied Camila, she stopped the pair of men and called out in a contented croon. "Camila! Look at me! See my newest slaves!"

Camila suddenly noticed Tasia's disheveled hair and Chaya's smug expression and the fact that Ariston was old in the wake of Corvina's young, robust slaves. She silently fumed inside. Corvina would notice these things. "I've new ones, too."

"Hmm," Corvina mused, grinning. "So, what're you doing out?"

"Shopping for a dress." Camila tried to prop her chin up higher and stare down her nose. Corvina would obviously have something to brag about, and she wanted to be ready for it.

"In the heat of the day? Not under a canopy?" Corvina chuckled. She lifted a fan and fluttered it against her face.

Camila smoothed out her gown. She was surprisingly at a loss for words. She usually knew what to say, but she just stared.

A smirk crossed Corvina's lips. "My father wouldn't stand for such a thing, walking in the heat." She fluttered the lashes above her deeply kohl-lined eyes and cupped her hand over her mouth, holding back a crooked smile.

Tasia was sympathetic. "Excuse me for my boldness," she interrupted.

Corvina let out a sound and pulled the curtain back wider. She stared haughtily at the slave.

Camila's brow rose, but she said nothing.

"In Camila's defense, it seems she's slender and fit in form, much healthier and prettier than most women, which I'm sure is an advantage over those being carried around in a litter."

Camila straightened, then pushed Tasia behind her. She stepped up to one of Corvina's slaves and traced a muscle in his arm.

A half-smile flitted across the young man's face, and he shuddered at her touch.

"Men like a woman whose body is fit." Her eyes slid over Covina's form.

Corvina frowned. "I'd be more concerned with the actions of my slaves. Yours might need some lessons in respect." She looked at Tasia with a raised brow. "She's quite unconventional and should've been taught some manners."

Camila pursed her lips, and her eyes narrowed. Then, she tossed a length of hair behind her. "I've no time for this. There's

105

cloth to buy, and I must be getting back. My mother's waiting for me."

Corvina nodded. "Yes, well, I need to get out of this heat. I'll see you next dinner."

Camila lifted her chin. "Until then."

Camila watched Corvina close the filmy, curtained windows of her canopy bed and turn away. Her eyes narrowed. The next dinner party couldn't come too soon for her.

After the litter disappeared into the crowded marketplace and Camila had a chance to recollect herself, she turned back to Chaya and Tasia. Her mouth tightened around the corners. "Never, will either of you ever speak so boldly in front of my friends, again. Do you hear me?" Her voice was a hiss.

Tasia and Chaya lowered their heads. "We won't."

A smile flitted across Camila's face. They better not, if they knew what was good for them.

She looked down the street. "There's the shop." She pointed to an ornate marble building with an arched doorway leading into it. "They have the best fabrics from the orient mother would approve of." Now, this was the right type of shop. Those slaves knew nothing about good fabric.

Chaya and Tasia sighed. "Yes, Miss," they both chanted in unison.

***

Chapter 15

Kalista searched one villa after another for at least a month and found nothing. She was getting discouraged. Her uncle must have been using a different name. No one knew anybody with her mother's family name. How many cobblestone streets could a person walk?

"Justus! I need you!" She called to him from across the unpaved street.

He was standing in front of a vine-covered brick villa with large, rectangular windows. He leaned against a stone rail that led to the door. He looked her way, but didn't respond. Instead, he smiled at a young woman with dark-hair who was next to him, playfully pushing him, her cream-colored tunic slipping over her shoulder.

He cupped his mouth over the young woman's ear and whispered something to her, ignoring Kalista.

Kalista noticed he'd put on a new toga with embroidered gold stripes on the lower edge and had sandals on she'd never seen before with leather straps that wound around and crossed over his calves. It was obvious he wanted to impress the girl he was with.

The young woman laughed, smoothing out her skirt. She leaned forward and whispered something, giggling.

Kalista made a face. She was tired of Justus spending all his time toying with this unpleasant girl. Basina was getting in the way of her searches for her family. The girl was loud, obnoxious and demanding, putting her own needs ahead everyone else. What did he see in her?

She plucked a long blade of grass next to her and chewed on the end, disgusted with what had been unfolding here in the last couple of days.

Kalista was sure Justus latched onto Basina because of her money and slaves. With her father recently deceased, he could marry her, without resistance. And yet, she was the most loud-mouthed annoying girl Kalista had ever met.

"Justus!" Kalista rolled her eyes. "I have to talk! Please!" She called out to him again, this time more insistently. She stood waiting for him, still holding the long stem of grass in her hand.

Kara S. McKenzie

He signaled to her, sending her an annoyed look. "Just a moment. I'll *be* there." He squeezed Basina's hand and whispered one more thing to her, grinning from ear to ear while he crossed the street to where Kalista stood.

Kalista was pacing back and forth on the street. She wiped the dampness from her neck, wishing it weren't so hot this day. She had so much to do. She threw the long grass stem on the ground and looked out over the city.

From the hill where they stood, the houses in Pompeii stretched out before them like pebbles on a beach. Larger hills loomed above them and the volcano spread its massive peak over the horizon. She wondered what ever happened to her family and where they were now.

Justus set his hands on his hips. "Give it up. You're not going to find them. Something must have happened. None of your relatives are anywhere in this place." He kicked at a rock on the path and watched it roll down the hill, until it bounced to a stop.

Kalista looked down the road where they were living. It was desolate today, not a sole in sight. A lone gull screamed over the villa in the square, sounding his angry cries above her. She felt lost and alone. Not even Justus was a comfort anymore. All the years of waiting, and now this. She'd not found one relative.

"But, I have to try. There must be one person who can help me. I can't give up. My family has to be around here, somewhere."

On a hill in the distance, a funeral procession was taking place. The faint sound of women wailing behind a line of mourners on their way to a burial ground drifted over the rooftops and down to the road where they stood. Kalista groaned, feeling as if time was slipping away. The depressing scene was a reminder that everyday she didn't find what she was looking for, the chances of it happening were getting more dismal. "My father will never take me back, and I've waited too long. I have to find them."

"But, your money's running out." Justus touched her hand. "And Gaius is there. He cares for you. I know he'd help, if you asked."

She snatched her hand from him as if burned. "I don't want him! I want to find my relatives, and I plan to keep looking until I do." She let out a breath and sat down on a large rock on the side of the road, placing her head in her hands.

108

Kalista's Hope

Gaius. Something gnawed at her deep inside when she thought of him. She wanted to forget him and kept trying to block him from her mind.

She got up again, not able to sit still. "Please. Just a little more time. Will you help, a little longer?" He had to. She had no one else.

She began to pace again on the road, the flowing wrap she carried dragging on the ground. She lifted it from the dust, shaking it and pulling it over her shoulders.

Justus sighed. "Basina doesn't approve, and I've asked her to be my wife. I can't keep supporting you. It won't work." He shook his head from side to side, looking as if he felt bad, but could do nothing about it.

Kalista turned sharply. "You asked *her* to marry you? What?" She looked shocked. "Justus, have you lost your mind? Can't you see that she's not right for you?" She couldn't believe that he would pick such a coarse girl to settle down with, when there were so many others who would be happy to have him.

He shook his head. "No. You're wrong. She'll be right. You'll see. And don't say anything else, because we are getting married, very soon."

Kalista sucked in a breath, shaking her head. "Oh Justus." It was all she was able to say. She looked toward the villa where Basina went inside. She was surprised she couldn't hear that loud, brash woman's voice through the brick walls.

"She's not what you think." He ran a hand along his tunic and pulled the wrap he was wearing closer around his shoulders. He tucked it into the gold clasp on his waist to secure it. "She *can* be a bit spirited now and then, but she treats me well."

Kalista didn't look convinced. "I think she's ridiculous and that you're really doing it for the money. Basina's rude, loud and obnoxious. And I don't like her."

Justus stammered. "Stop. You know I wouldn't marry just for the money. How can you say something like that?"

She didn't speak again, but scuffed the ground with her sandal and looked down.

He frowned. "Do you ever believe you're wrong?"

"What?" Kalista looked shocked. "Sometimes, I do."

He shook his head and looked defeated. "I don't want to argue. You can think what you want." He turned and stalked back across the street grabbing hold of the stone rail and running

109

Kara S. McKenzie

his hands along it as he passed on by. He went through the arched doorway leaving Kalista on the street alone.

She gritted her teeth, angry that he used to listen to her, and now all he did was blame her. Her time would be ending soon in this place, and she hadn't found any relatives.

She let out a long breath and looked back over the city. The sky above it was turning dark. One lone star appeared. An ache settled deep inside her. Soon there would be other stars, and they would swallow this one up. Just like her, swallowed up by the people in the city of Pompeii, one in thousands.

She wondered what would happen now. Who would she stay with when her money ran out, as there would definitely be no place for her with Justus after the wedding? She was sure Basina didn't care what happened to her, and she'd be out on the streets if she didn't find anyone else to stay with.

What a mess she'd found herself in. No way back to Rome, and no relative in sight. What was she going to do? There was nothing else she could do. She had to find them.

***

Chapter 16

Gaius followed Tasia down the marble hallway, eying the artwork on the walls. Despite the bold, colorful designs, he sensed something oppressive in the house.

They stopped in the atrium, a large central room, surrounded by four bedrooms, a dining room and a living room. Even with the elaborate décor, shining white marble walls and intricately carved moldings, there was something lacking. The room was bare and cold, silent as the statues placed strategically about the room. He could understand why Kallie didn't like spending her time here.

The sound of Gaius' sandaled feet echoed as he made his way across the patterned stone floor to where Kallie's father was.

The young slave woman took Gaius to an arched doorway leading into one of the bedrooms. There were two, tall columns at the entrance where she pushed back a thin, filmy green curtain.

Because of the heavy rain clouds blocking the sun, there was very little light coming through the small, rectangular opening in the middle of the atrium. Gaius had a difficult time seeing anything but shadows in the room.

"How is he? Someone said he's ill?"

Tasia turned. "He's been struggling with a recent tragedy in their family and hasn't taken the news well." She paused a moment before going in.

"It's that bad?" Gaius looked concerned.

She nodded. "One of his daughters died in a tragic accident, and he's not been the same since."

"Died?" he stammered, suddenly pale. "Which one?" He'd never forgive himself for letting Kallie go, if anything had happened to her on the way to Pompeii.

He put his hand on the column next to him, his fingers curling around the grooves in it.

"The daughter of his first wife. I guess when her friend Justus' father died and the house collapsed, it fell on her, too. They didn't find the body, though. Justus left to go south before anyone could speak to him."

She eyed him solemnly and then turned to look into the smaller room again.

Kara S. McKenzie

It took Gaius a few seconds to make sense of what he heard, and when he did, the pallor in his face returned. He breathed a sigh of relief.

So, this is how she got past her father. He'd been right in his assumptions about her. She'd found a way to escape the arranged marriage and her father's wrath without a hitch. He shook his head at the thought of it.

Then he groaned. Great…he'd given her his word he'd not say anything, and wondered if he'd be able to keep his promise. She'd know if he told anyone.

He followed Tasia into the corner of the dark room where Terentius was lying on a pallet underneath heavy, woolen blankets. It took a while for his eyes to adjust to the dark, to see the still form lying beside him.

Tasia backed out of the room, leaving the two of them.

"Terentius Neo?" Gaius tugged gently at the covers encircling the man.

There was a deep groan that came from underneath the woolen blanket. Terentius rolled over. His eyes were sunken hollows. "I told you I wanted no one disturbing me." He growled as he lifted the blanket. His brows furrowed when he saw Gaius. "Who are you?"

Gaius sat on the low, wooden bench next to the bed. He rested his arm on the upper portion that rolled back like a scroll. "Your wife sent for me. She wanted me to help settle some of your affairs. I'm the lawyer."

He looked around the room, noticing statues of gods placed strategically in each corner on marble tables and shelves. Their muscled bodies were meant to depict power and a certain mystical quality in them, and yet to Gaius, they looked small and oddly obscure. He guessed they were put there as a measure of protection.

He sighed. "She thought you might need me to come."

Terentius withdrew deeper under his covers. "Hmph! She doesn't think the physician can heal me."

"I'm sure something can be done." Gaius voice was assuring. He said a quick, silent prayer.

Terentius looked at him with cold, dark eyes.

"What's wrong? Do you hurt?" Gaius didn't think Terentius looked physically ill.

112

Kalista's Hope

Terentius pulled the covers tighter around him. His robe slipped down over his arm, revealing the colored border of a Rome consul.

Gaius sighed. The rich and poor were all alike when it came to sickness and death. No one escaped because of status.

"If it were only that easy." Terentius shook his head.

"What do you mean?"

"There's nothing wrong with my body. It's much worse than that, a sickness of my soul."

Gaius looked concerned. "So, the parchment might not be necessary at this time?" He wasn't sure why they called him to come.

Terentius shook his head. "I didn't say that. People die of broken hearts all the time, and the way I feel, I have to make sure things are in order."

Gaius put his hand on Terentius' shoulder. "Because of your daughter?"

Terentius nodded reluctant. "Yes. But, what truly breaks my heart is that I never gave her a chance and blamed her when her mother died. I never offered protection to the gods for her...ever."

There was silence. And then he whispered. "She was my former wife's child. How could I have done such a thing? Gabriella would've never wanted me to have treated her that way."

Gaius patted his shoulder, wanting very much to tell Terentius that his daughter was still very much alive. Yet, if her father found out what she did, he might never forgive her. He might even harm her in some way.

Gaius realized he had to protect Kallie at all costs, even if it meant her rightful inheritance would go to Domnica. He prayed she'd find her mother's family in Pompeii.

A chill descended over the room. Gaius noticed the lack of décor in the tiny, boxlike space, devoid of the lively frescos and tiled floors of the adjacent rooms. There was hardly any furniture in the room, other than the bed and the low bench he sat on, and a small nightstand. He wondered if it was Terentius' way of punishing himself.

"Before you sign the papers, I think we should talk first."

Terentius sighed. "Nothing you say could change anything."

113

Kara S. McKenzie

"Maybe. But, sometimes to see the light, the dark's necessary." Gaius took a seat next to the bed.

"I've definitely had my fill of that." Terentius looked as if he had little hope, yet seemed to draw a certain confidence from Gaius' keen blue eyes. "I'll listen, then we'll get the words on the parchment taken care of."

Gaius nodded, hoping he might help this man. "So...tell me about what you believe." He eyed the gods in the corners of the rooms.

Terentius sunk further under stark, thin covers. "The supremacy of Rome of course, and obedience to the state authorities, and the Emperor. What else is there? You're Roman. You'd know this."

"I meant your spiritual beliefs?" Gaius encouraged him with a nod.

Terentius sighed. "To appease our gods of course, a frustrating affair with hundreds of them."

Gaius nodded. "I thought as much."

They both turned when they heard loud voices and banging sounds coming from the adjacent room. Someone didn't sound happy.

Gaius got up to check on the disturbance.

Terentius motioned for Gaius to stay seated. He sighed. "It's more than likely, Camila. It will end soon. Go on...we can still talk."

Gaius shook his head and smiled. Did everyone in the Neo household have a temper? He wondered if Camila was anything like Kallie. What an interesting place this estate would be with the two of them under the same roof.

"Let's keep talking." He bent his head to listen.

***

114

Chapter 17

"Stand right here. I told you both, I'd have no more of it!" Camila hissed the words through her teeth. She glared red-faced, at Tasia and Chaya. These worthless slaves of Kalista's were making fun of her again. It was the last time she'd put up with it. They'd certainly pay for what they were putting her though.

When she thought of how disrespectful they were and the way they were looking at her, she grabbed a wooden tray full of fruits and meats off the dining room table and flung it at them, not caring that she'd ruin a whole morning meal. "You think it's funny!"

Both Chaya and Tasia shrieked and tried to dart out of the way.

The pieces of food sailed through the air and hit the front of Tasia's woolen tunic and then dropped to the patterned floor. The tray careened in another direction and clattered wildly when it hit, tumbling a couple times before it came to a stop. It just missed bumping into the base of one of their many statues.

Camila was red with fury. "Now, see what you did! You almost broke the sculpture!" She ignored the fact that it was she who threw the platter and that it came nowhere near to doing any actual damage to the piece of artwork.

Tasia stared at her tunic in shocked silence and began to try and wipe the stains from it. Her mouth fell open. She looked at Camila confused, as if she just learned the full extent of her mistress' temper.

Other servants scrambled to collect the food bits and wipe any evidence from the tiled floor, while trying to stay out of the fray.

Camila let out a breath, a frown posturing her brow. She didn't like losing her temper like that, but believed the slaves deserved every bit of it.

She straightened her shoulders and lifted her chin. "Hmph! Serves you both right." She smoothed out her own silken gown and took a step back, lifting the hem of her gown off the floor.

She pointed at the front of Tasia's tunic. "Now, you've ruined your clothes. And you can't afford to do that." She shook her head. "My parents pay for those. I hope you're happy with all the trouble you've caused."

She took a seat on a cushioned chair with legs in the shape of lion's paws. One of the slaves in a nearby corner rushed over and poured her a drink and handed the chalice to her.

She didn't look at the slave, but took it in her hand and raised the container to her lips, taking a sip. She held it in her lap and then smiled wickedly at Tasia and Chaya. Her voice had an edge to it. "Get your things, all of them. It looks like you'll need to see for yourself what happens to disobedient slaves."

When the servants finished cleaning the area, they backed off and slunk into corners of the room. They didn't seem to want to be anywhere near Camila during another of her fits of rage.

Chaya looked a bit shaken, but held herself in check. "We meant no disrespect, Camila. "Please. It won't happen again." She sighed, wondering what their punishment would be.

Camila smiled, amused. A surge of power shot through her, and she liked the feeling of it. She took another drink, fingering the floral designs on the cup, all the while conjuring up a plan to retaliate against the two women who had lowered themselves to the floor.

It was gratifying to see these high-handed slaves bowed down to her. Her mouth curved as she watched them. Very soon she'd relish in another sport with them. Let them see what their behavior would get them.

She put the chalice back on the stand and adjusted the folds of her gown, and then lifted her arm and pointed at them. "Go! And if you're not back by the time the sundial's reached mid-day, you'll regret it!"

Her eyes danced when both girls dashed out of the room without a word. They underestimated their young mistress' power. She was going to make sure those women would never do anything to her again.

***

Out of sight, and within the confines of their room, Chaya and Tasia both gathered the few possessions they owned. They took one last look around the tiny space connected to Kalista's empty room.

Chaya's face paled. She felt a lump forming in her throat. "What do you think Camila's going to do?"

Tasia reached out and placed a hand on her friend's arm. "Don't worry. Whatever it is, I'm sure her mother will need to

116

Kalista's Hope

approve it. We're valuable to them, and Domnica would want to keep us. It'll be all right. You'll see."

Chaya looked doubtful, but nodded. "I certainly hope so, because, she surely didn't act as if we were staying."

Tasia nodded reluctantly. "I guess we'll see. I wish we'd been more careful. I just never thought she'd go this far."

She changed her tunic and gathered up the rest of what little she had and motioned to Chaya. "I'm ready. Let's go. We don't want to keep her waiting."

Chaya inclined her head. "It looks like we'll see what she has planned now."

***

Chapter 18

"You're a Christian, aren't you?" Terentius eyed Gaius with interest. He suddenly looked every bit the Roman consul.

Gaius nodded.

Although, Terentius was more or less a figurehead in the government, Gaius knew the man had connections with those in power. He wondered what might happen to him after admitting his Christian faith to such an influential man.

Terentius sat up. He lowered his voice, watching the door. "I have friends I've known all my life who I've respected greatly. I recently found them to be tied to this sect, and they admitted to being believers. But, I don't understand it. All I know is that the sect seems to be growing."

"There are new followers every day, rich, poor…men, women…people of all races." Gaius nodded. "So many people from so many different backgrounds, all with the same central belief."

Terentius shook his head. "I've seen it, and often wondered about it. When it comes to religion, we Romans have difficulty coming together as one. I can't even remember half of the gods and what I need to do to appease them."

Gaius sighed. "It's true, there is unity in the Christian's central belief, but we definitely need to keep asking God how to solve the disagreements we do have."

Terentius was silent. He rubbed the slight beard on his chin. "I suppose people will argue, no matter what they believe. No one can get away from that."

Gaius nodded. This was true. "So, did you know who Jesus was and what happened to him?"

Terentius hesitated. "A prophet? A Jew? Gabriella used to try and tell me about him, but what she said sounded like a bunch of babble."

"Your former wife?"

"Yes."

Gaius acknowledged him with a lift of his chin. "Well, I don't know if she told you, but he spoke of the afterlife. Do you ever wonder what is going to happen to you when you die?"

Terentius shrugged. "Not really. I treated Kalista miserably, and my life has been self-serving. I suppose if there *is*

Kalista's Hope

an afterlife, I stand little chance on my own merits going somewhere good when I die."

Gaius wasn't sure how to make Terentius understand. He struggled for the right words to say. "What if you were told truth could be explained? Would you want to know what it really was?"

"Is such a thing possible?" Terentius chuckled.

Gaius shook his head.

Terentius shrugged. "I suppose if it were possible to know what it was…anyone would want to."

"So, do you have time to listen to what I have to say?"

"Time?" Terentius sighed. "I have more than I can bear."

***

Kalista entered one last villa and inquired in the front room.

She made her way over wooden floorboards to a man standing next to a marble table stacked with scrolls and parchment. He was sorting through them and placing them in piles. He was wearing the coarse, homespun clothing of the lower class, so she assumed he wasn't the owner of the stately villa.

"Could I ask you something?"

The man looked up. He eyed her curiously and smiled. "Sure. I don't know if I can give you the answer you want, but I'll try." He put down the wax tablet and stylus he held in his hand and turned to her. He wiped his hands on the front of his tunic, which had been torn at one time, but patched up neatly. "So, what is your question?"

She repeated the words she'd come to know quite well, and felt almost rote saying them. "Did you know a woman named Gabriella Cato, who married Terentius Neo? Is there anyone you know who lives here who could have been related?"

The man thought a moment, then shook his head. "Sorry, I've never heard of her. I wish I could help. The owner's name of this place is Cassius Gallus and his wife is Cyra." He looked as if he wished he could've provided her with more information.

That didn't help Kalista, as she didn't know the first names of any of her relatives. She was never allowed to ask. She took a step back and gazed out one of the windows, sighing. Was every one of her relatives dead? Wasn't there anyone who could tell her anything about her mother? She'd waited so long and tried so hard, and now, all she was finding in this city were dead ends. It wasn't fair.

119

Kara S. McKenzie

She turned to leave, holding back tears that threatened to drop. The search had laid a melancholy trail over her heart. She hesitated briefly to take one last look around the room.

Nothing. Not a trace. The name Paquius Proculus was painted in letters on one of the walls. "Do you know if this name might lead me to a clue?"

The man shook his head. "No, that's me. I only run the place for the people, now. I have no long lost relatives."

"I see." Kalista let out a long, slow breath.

And then her eyes lit on a fresco on the wall of the Villa. What caught her eye was not the woman in the painting with the large, cinnamon eyes or fiery hair the color of her own, or the man next to her, but the earrings, which dangled from the woman's ears.

Kalista's hands shook, as she took the box containing her mother's earrings from a small pouch slung over her shoulder. She held one of the gems up to the painting and choked back tears. The woman was wearing the same ones!

The likeness in the painting was significant, too. It had to be her mother, or a close relative. And the man standing next to her was undoubtedly her father, in his younger years. He had the same wide, dark eyes and slight mustache and beard, yet he was younger and there was a soft look in his eyes, one she'd never known. He was leaning close to the woman and holding a scroll in his hand.

Kalista studied the painting closer. The woman was pretty with a sweet, gentle face. Her hair was coiled above her head and one long braid slipped over her shoulder. She was holding a wax tablet and a stylus. Kalista was sure it was a message to anyone viewing the painting, sharing the fact that the woman liked to write.

Kalista studied the woman and man in the painting. She could feel the love between them and their dependence upon each other. It made her feel special, as if she were part of it.

Suddenly, her heart swelled with joy. The woman and the man in the painting had to be her mother and father. Someone here would know and would be able to help. And she might finally meet a relative from her mother's side of the family. She couldn't wait to talk to the owner.

***

Gaius spoke quietly, as Terentius listened. This was their third session, together. Their talks proved to be interesting, but

Kalista's Hope

Terentius still was reticent to listen to too much at one time. Light from the doorway filtered in through the curtain from the atrium. The sun must have come out. "There *is* a God, but not anything like the ones you know."

Terentius waved his hand. "Yes...another god. I see." He looked annoyed, staring at the imprint of Bacchus' face, engraved into a stone tile protruding from the sidewall next to him. Bacchus was screaming, his beard curled beneath his mouth and hair wild around his facem laden with fruit.

Gaius turned from it. "Not *just* another one. The One true One." He prayed a quick prayer that Terentius would understand the difference.

"Hmph." Terentius picked up one of the small gods, a keeper of the gate sitting on the stand beside him. "All I need, another god."

Gaius sat up straighter. "But, the God I follow *is* different. You said it yourself. The Christian God can bring unity to the ones who follow his Word, at least if they are truly following it the way Jesus said to."

Terentius looked interested. He put the god back on the stand.

"For true believers. We've learned the way to connect with God in our hearts. This means Romans, Jews, slaves, Greeks, women or anyone who seeks him, a unity which transcends all races and people."

"Wait a minute." Terentius wagged his finger in the air, the sleeve of his toga slipping down his arm. "I've seen the riots and disagreements within the sect. It's a far cry from unity."

"It's true that some use Christianity as a vice, for their own advancement. They may use the name, but don't follow Jesus teachings. Him and his followers promoted love, peace, humility and all that's good, what Christians who love God strive for. If they aren't doing this, then they are Christians in name only, no different than a thief posing as the owner of the home he's stealing from.

Terentius pushed a pillow behind him and propped himself up. He looked as if what Gaius said might be of importance to him. "I've seen some Christians in Rome, who have nothing in common, yet treat each other like family. I can't say it doesn't intrigue me, as I've never observed so many different classes and races of people coming together as one. Deference to an emperor is required, but you people freely give

121

yourself to this God, which has also been a puzzle to me."
Terentius leaned on his elbow. "Tell me why this is so?"

Gaius voice was steady. His eyes never wavered when he spoke. "He wasn't made by human hands, but he made the world and everything in it. He's without stain or blemish."

He stood up and paced the floor, stopping near a fresco that depicted a man in a purple robe, with a wreath encircling his head. "Just as the emperor demands obeisance, there's one thing our God asks of us."

Terentius chuckled. "I assumed as such. Nothing comes without a price."

Gaius explained further. "When we meet him in the afterlife, he asks that we be pure, perfect. He's as uncorrupt as gold, and anything less would defile him. This is the cost of which I speak. We must be perfect." He moved away from the painting and sat on the curved bench next to Terentius. He reached down and tied a strap of his sandal that had come undone.

Terentius frowned. "But that's impossible. No one for that matter, not even yourself, as sincere as you seem, has the ability to rise to that level. Your God attaches a cost to the afterlife so pricey even the richest of kings couldn't afford it." He sighed.

Gaius smiled. "It does seem insurmountable. But, I tell you, I'm certain I'll stand without a drop of sin before this God, pure and without fault in the afterlife. You may not think so, but I know it's possible. And, you're right in saying, I can't pay the cost."

"What?" Terentius placed his hands on his temples and closed his eyes. "You don't make any sense. I'm sure this is what they mean about the foolishness of your religion. There are discrepancies in what you say."

Gaius leaned forward. "No, Terentius, there aren't any discrepancies."

Terentius looked skeptical. "But you say your God requires you to pay a cost to enter into the afterlife, one in which you can't pay. So, how do you propose you'll stand before him someday, when you're unable to meet these requirements? You said it yourself, that you couldn't pay the cost."

Gaius sat on the chair next the bed and held the edge of it. "Because the God I speak of found a way to pay it *for* me."

122

Kalista's Hope

Terentius cocked an eyebrow. The look on his face was unconvinced. "I still don't understand. How can anything like this happen?"

Gaius looked him straight in the eye. "At the cross. I saw the conviction of others who told us about Jesus, and I found the answers I was looking for."

Terentius took hold of the sleeve Gaius' robe. "You believe this, and you're Roman?" He stared at Gaius, puzzled.

Gaius shrugged. "We spend our lives trying to understand truth or find a god to satisfy us, but we fall short every time. Yet, with Jesus, we find all of our searching was worthless without him. There's a path we can take that will lead us to him."

Terentius' ears perked. "Tell me. I'm tired. I want to know this path."

***

Chapter 19

"I wish to sell two of my slaves," Camila announced loudly.

Chaya and Tasia shrunk from her grip. They cringed while eying the room in Nero's ornate palace. The people there reclined on swayed back chairs at low tables. They drank heavily from oversized chalices, and grinned while they wiped excess dribbles from their mouths and chin. Others draped in filmy tunics staggered to the music of minstrels, giggling hysterically, as if they'd been carousing most of the day. The palace echoed with laughter.

Nero's slaves showed little emotion, going about their tasks, with traces of fear hidden in their solemn expressions. They eyed Chaya and Tasia sympathetically.

A tall, heavy-set man in a blue robe with large pieces of gold jewelry swinging from his neck came forward. He took hold of Tasia's hair and ran his hands through it, nodding. He smiled approvingly and then instructed both girls to turn round for him.

Both Chaya and Tasia reluctantly complied.

A triumphant grin spread over Camila's face as both girls moved slowly under the gaze of Nero's attendant. Ha! That'll teach those worthless slaves. She lifted her fingers to her mouth and held back a giggle.

The man reached out and put his hand on Chaya's arm holding it there. He grinned like a dog eating a meal. It was obvious he'd overextended himself on the wine that seemed to flow freely in the room.

Slaves held rich-looking drinks and platters of food and carried them to the tables where people were eating, while an incessant hum of conversation filled the great marble dining area. The people there seemed oblivious to the two slave girls.

Chaya backed away at the man's touch.

He smiled. "Nero might have use for them. I will consider them for a good price."

Camila's face lit, reveling in the terror on both Chaya and Tasia's faces. Everyone knew the unpredictability of Nero's actions and how he treated his slaves.

Kalista's Hope

"How much?" She bargained. The girls would pay dearly for their insolence, And she wouldn't have to deal with them anymore.

"Fifty denarii for them both."

Camila made a face. "Only Fifty?"

The man took a drink, and his eyes swept over her with a lecherous grin. "Nero doesn't have to bargain, foolish girl. And you might find yourself in his slave's quarters too, if you're not careful."

He studied her more closely and reached out, sliding his fingers over the long braid of white, blonde hair that draped over her shoulder. "Remember this next time you frequent the palace. Fifty denarii and no more."

Camila's brow wrinkled. She pulled her shoulders back and lifted her chin haughtily, yanking her braid away from his grasp, but couldn't hide the fear creeping into her. She shuddered to think of him or Nero putting either of their filthy hands on her. "Fifty will be fine."

Her fingers trembled as he put the money in her hand, slightly grazing hers with his own.

She quickly pulled her hand away. She gave Chaya and Tasia over to him and left. If her joke backfired, and she had to spend any amount of time in that repulsive, disagreeable Emperor's palace, the whole scenario might not be so funny.

She looked back at her former slaves, who stared at her. Their eyes were large, in the wake of her leaving. She rarely felt any sympathy for her family's slaves when they were given consequences for their actions, especially disobedient ones, but this time, a tinge of guilt ran through her. After that man had looked at her the way he did and had threatened to take her to Nero, it stirred a nerve in her, and she almost felt like going back for them.

But instead, she made her way to the street, and pushed aside her short-lived feelings of remorse.

After she got in the cart with Ariston, who was waiting on the cobblestone street for her, she decided to put the whole affair out of her mind.

Hmph! If either of them hadn't been so disrespectful, they wouldn't have ended up at the palace. It was their fault, not hers. They'd been warned, but chose to continue their pranks even when she'd repeatedly told them to stop. They'd been too

125

bold with her and took too many liberties, more than a slave should. And they needed to learn a lesson.

She, on the other hand, had done nothing to deserve the treatment she'd gotten from that lowlife of Nero. She was not even close to the same caliber as those worthless women. No one owned her, and she balked at the idea that they thought they could.

She wished she could find a way to get back at that unruly man who had no right to treat her as he had. But, for now, she'd have to leave well enough alone. She'd gotten out of there with her life intact, and she accomplished what she set out to do. The deal had been made, and there was nothing she could do about it now.

"Let's go, Ariston." She waved a hand at him. "I want to get home."

Ariston clucked to the mules and the cart jolted forward and started down the street.

Camila held her hands in her lap to keep them from trembling. She gripped the edge of the cart to steady herself.

What was done was done, she thought. The slaves were gone and would find out where their disobedience got them, even if it was a little harsh. Her mother wouldn't mind, and her father didn't care about anything.

***

Chapter 20

"He told people, *he* was the way," Gaius said. "When Jesus took the punishment, by dying on the cross, he did it to take our place."

Terentius chuckled nervously. He wrapped the covers on his bed closer around him. "But the Roman soldiers, surely, *they* took his life?"

"No," Gaius protested. "He *gave* his life. People saw him alive afterward. Only God could come back from the dead."

Terentius shook his head, not quite comprehending, but remembered Gabriella and what she'd told him.

"Terentius, it's truth. You can believe it. He is the one true God. You need his forgiveness for what you did to your daughter and for the other sins committed in your life. Your statues of stone have done nothing for you. But, he could. If you believe that he died for your sin and rose from the grave, then you *will* be saved. *That* is the way."

***

Tired of arguments, and of pain, Terentius remembered Gabriella's last words. "Believe in the Christ. He *is* the way for you…I'll be waiting…please, believe."

Suddenly, it was making sense. All the things his wife told him. If he were to believe it, too, he could have what she and Gaius had, peace, and the hope of eternal life and seeing his darling wife who he thought he'd lost forever.

He bowed his head and made a profession of faith, repentant for what he'd done in his life and asking for help from this unseen God, immediately feeling a sense of relief and freedom inside. What a difference it was, knowing the way was the Christ.

Immediately, he got up from the bed. He called for one of his slaves, while Gaius stood watching him.

"Terentius?" Gaius went to him. "What do you plan to do?"

Terentius pointed to the household gods lining the wall. "I've realized these won't be necessary anymore. These gods haven't given me anything but problems. I see something I should have done long ago."

"You're getting rid of them?"

"Why not? What good are they?"

Gaius nodded, a smile lighting his face. "You *do* see."

"Yes." Terentius pointed at the idols, as a slave came into the room. "Take all them, and smash them."

The slave looked afraid, questioning meekly. "Master, have you lost your mind?"

"My mind's more steady than it's ever been." Terentius tipped his head forward. "There'll be changes from now on in this home. Like I said, smash them."

Gaius could tell that the man felt freedom for the first time in his life.

"But master, what will Domnica do?" The slave's brow creased.

Terentius shrugged his shoulders. Then he chuckled. "I'm not sure I wish to find out."

Gaius' brow curved upward. "Hmm. I suppose, it looks as if it's a good time to finish the paperwork I came to do and make my escape." He smiled.

Terentius nodded. And then, he suddenly winced in pain, a wounded look in his eyes.

Gaius couldn't imagine what he was upset about. "What is it? All should be well."

"Kalista. What've I done?" Terentius lowered his head, his face turning an ashen color. "She didn't know the way before she died."

His hands shook, and he lifted them in front of him. "I wouldn't listen. Oh, now she'll never know…because of me! What's become of her?" He let out a sob.

Gaius shook his head. "No. Terentius. There's still hope. I know something I must to tell you."

Terentius took his arm. "But she's dead. I can't bring her back now, to tell her."

Gaius shook his head. "But, you're wrong. There is a way for her, too."

"What're you saying?"

Gaius' look was one of guilt. "I couldn't tell you, because she wanted a way out, and I was afraid for her safety. She told me not to tell. I'm breaking a promise." He hoped Kalista wouldn't be too mad at him, but now everything had changed. Her father would not be the same man anymore.

"What are you saying, Gaius?" Terentius was perplexed.

Kalista's Hope

Gaius sighed. "She's not dead. She went to look for her mother's family in Pompeii."

Terentius grasped Gaius' arm, this time tighter. "Pompeii? She's alive?"

Gaius nodded.

Terentius looked incredulous and let out a breath. "So, it's not too late." And then he whispered. "There's still a way for her."

The pallor suddenly returned to his face. "I've the chance to change things. I must go to her, as soon as I can." He pulled himself from the bedside. "But, there's business I'm obligated to first in Rome, and after that, I'll leave as soon as I can to find her."

"And I'll go with you. I want to see her, too."

Terentius turned, his eyes square on Gaius' face. His expression was filled with wonder when he saw the tenderness in Gaius' eyes. He smiled. "So, you find my daughter favorable?"

Gaius shook his head. "Despite some of her hard-headed ways."

Terentius laughed. "Enough to go with me?"

Gaius eyebrows knit together for a brief second, and then a glow emanated from him, knowing his heart and how full it was for her. He figured he wouldn't give up on her, until she came to see things his way. "I will. Now, let's draw up those papers. Maybe we can go and something can be done to convince her of the truth."

***

Kalista fingered the stylus and folded piece of parchment her Aunt Cyra had given her. Her mother used this very writing tool once, and now it was hers to keep. It was the same one in the painting.

She was alone in one of the bedrooms of the villa. Her eyes were drawn to an oil lamp on a small stand next to the bed where she reclined. The fire flickered and rose upward. Light spread wide from the single flame, filling the whole expanse of the dark room. She'd never noticed before how far reaching the glow could be from such a tiny spark of fire.

She smiled as she eyed the colorful room, artwork dancing in the shimmers of light from the lamp. Scenes of gardens ripe with fruit, gave the paintings a rich full feeling, which is how she felt, having found her way to her relative's home.

Her mother *was* the woman in the painting on the wall, along with her father at a very young age. And at one time, they resided in this very place. Terentius and Gabriella Neo. His uncle's family name was now Cassius and no longer the same as her mother, as he had taken the more prestigious family name of his wife. Those working for him were unaware of the change in his family name. When she'd seen Paquius Proculus' name on the wall, she assumed it was the man in the painting, until the earrings gave the mystery away. It was the Neo painting, instead.

Kalista lifted the parchment she held and read the words for the hundredth time, letting them sink in, cherishing the message. Written down by her mother were the same words Gaius tried to explain to her. But, she'd not listened. Yet, seeing the truth laid out before her through her mother's own words, this time, it was different and seemed right to her.

Her mother was a Christian, along with her aunt and uncle, and in her mother's hand were copied the Good News of Jesus.

She began to read, and this time to try to understand. Whatever her mother was offering her, she'd at least make an effort to learn.

The truth of the words sank deep in her heart, as she read them over and over, straining to understand what her mother professed to know. A simple opening of her heart and acceptance of this God would take her to eternity someday and free her from the bondage she couldn't seem to escape. The words were bold and expressed confidence, nothing like she'd ever known, professing promise and assurance in a simple prayer of faith.

She sighed. Had her daily offerings, prayers and rote chants to her own gods done anything for her? Had they answered any of the questions she repeatedly brought before them?

She shook her head sadly and began to weep. No. Nothing she believed in made a single shred of difference in her life, or led to answers she so desperately searched for. All they managed to do was cause her more fear and pain than she cared to endure.

Would this God be different? Surely, she could trust in one both Gaius and her mother believed in? Surely, neither of them would attempt to lead her astray.

When it became clear to her what she needed to do, Kalista bowed her head, her heart pounding loudly in her chest.

Kalista's Hope

"Lord, I believe in you and in what you did, and I ask you to take my sin. I'm sorry for it. Help me be what my mother was, a follower of you."

Tears blurred her vision and slipped quietly down her cheeks. A certain sense of relief spread over her, and she suddenly felt the ache inside her lighter than she'd ever known.

She stared out the window of the upper room, eying the heavy, chiseled stone statues sweeping the city in hundreds, her people's gods, immovable, lifeless, cast by human hands. They suddenly seemed insignificant delusions and cheap imitations. The oppressive gods who threatened her spirit and mind daily in the past, seemed of no consequence now.

A new peace swept over her.

She bowed her head and prayed again. "Thank you."

All at once, hope rose within her, as she pondered how God reached her through her sweet mother from the grave, giving her security, a passage someday to his beautiful place in heaven.

She smiled. God opened her heart and freed it with one prayer.

She laughed, her eyes sparkling with truth. The weight that hung so heavily upon her shoulders was miraculously gone.

It was her father who held the words in his hands in the painting, so she figured he'd heard them before. But, he'd chosen to not accept them. If he only had. She sighed.

But, she would tell Justus! He had to know. She'd go to him now and see if he might accept this message, too.

***

Chapter 21

Tasia had yet to meet up with Nero. She sighed with relief that the palace was as large as it was. There were hundreds of slaves working in his palace, many of them beautiful, young women. So, for the most part, her and Chaya went unnoticed.

Tasia put a plate of vegetables on the table. She moved in silence, drawing as little attention to herself as possible, having learned in the home to keep inconspicuous, hiding in the shadows and only coming out when ordered to do so. If for any reason, Nero noticed her, it wouldn't be a good thing.

Tasia lowered her eyes when one of the male slaves entered the room carrying food on a tray. Antonius. She couldn't help noticing his smile, before she averted her eyes.

He leaned down. "Do you need anything?" He adjusted the sleeve on his arms.

Tasia sighed. She liked the looks of this man with his chiseled face and dark hair, but the lives of slaves were too unpredictable, and it wouldn't do to get her hopes up. "Thank you. We have what we need." She turned away.

He smelled of strong bath salts. She could barely hear his voice, but felt his presence behind her. "I wish I could find a way to get you out of this place."

Tasia looked at him warily. She whispered. "Nothing can be done. We both know this."

"But, maybe there will be a time for it."

She stopped working a moment and watched as he left the room. How was it possible to keep living in in a place like this that afforded no hope? Why was she chosen for such a lot in life? What had she done to deserve it?

"Tasia!" The head slave screamed at her. "What are you doing, standing there? Get back to the kitchen!"

Tasia rubbed her hands on her tunic, and then took quick steps past a tall, matronly woman with the hard-edged face. She tipped her head down as she went under the arched doorway and into a steamy, hot room with no windows where starchy smelling pots bubbled with pottage and meat lying in strips ready to cook, along with chopped vegetables.

There were oil lamps set around, and fire from the hearth was kept continually lit. The shadows from the light skipped and

Kalista's Hope

hopped across the dark brick walls and arched doorways of the room.

Tasia placed fruit on plates, arranging it in patterns, trying to resist the temptation to shove a grape into her mouth. Although she felt faint and her stomach rumbled, she held back. The consequences were too great for such a thing. Smaller portions for the slaves would be afforded later.

She might see Chaya at night, when the slaves took to their pallets for sleep. She smiled at the thought of her friend working with cloth in the back rooms. At least she was relatively safe from some of the difficulties faced by most of the slaves, and Nero wouldn't be spending time in her company. The man was a crazed lunatic, and Tasia wanted nothing to do with him.

***

"You…what?" Justus got up, rubbing his hands together and began to pace. His fingers brushed against the flat stone base that surrounded the statue of the god, Apollo, he'd been sitting on.

The town outside Pompeii was quiet, save for a few birds in some olive trees in the courtyard where Kalista was staying.

Justus stopped pacing. His thin fingers tapped against the folds of his toga. "You can't be serious?"

Kalista nodded. "I *am*. I found it in my mother's writings." She held the words on the stylus against her chest and looked up at him from the bench where she sat.

He groaned. "But, it's ludicrous! I never thought you'd be taken in by such nonsense."

When he saw the serious look on her face, he laughed.

"Justus, please…it's not nonsense. I know." She pulled her wrap tighter about her. There was breeze, and the air was cool from the sea.

He laughed again, this time harder. "All because of a letter from a long dead mother who probably never read a book in her life."

Kalista couldn't hold back the fury she felt had risen inside her. Her cheeks began to flame. "You're not even paying attention! You used to at least listen to me!" She felt a tinge of guilt at her outburst, but believed it justified, because of the way he was treating her.

Justus dropped his gaze to hers. He let out a sound. "I listened to you, *when* you spoke with intelligence."

Her dark eyes flashed with anger at his insult. "Do you really think I can't think for myself anymore?" She shoved her

133

hair behind her in one large sweep, despite the still, small voice within her, urging her to silence.

"I thought Christians were supposed to be sweet and demure and non-judgmental?" Justus grinned.

Kalista bit back another retort and then sighed. *"You know* I've never been sweet, demure or non-judgmental. That'll surely not change overnight. But, one thing I do know, I don't have to *be* anything, for this God to love me. I only have to believe my sins are paid for and that he'll take me to my mother, someday. That's the hope I have. Justus, the peace is unreal."

For a moment, Justus looked almost interested, and then he shook his head. He threw his hands in the air. "I'm done. I've had enough this."

He turned, shaking his head. Then he stalked off to the villa and went inside a large, wooden door, slamming it behind him.

Kalista stared at the arched passageway in disbelief, remembering a time she did the same thing to Gaius. She was beginning to understand that being a Christian might not be the easiest path to take, and yet if given the choice again, she'd gladly make the same decision all over again.

***

Basina rolled her eyes and laughed. "I think your friend's mad. It's good she'll finally be out of your life. She's been a thorn in your side for a long time."

Justus nodded, although not without some uneasiness. Some of the things Kalista said were difficult to put from his mind.

He shrugged his shoulders, wary of his own response. "It's hard to say. She might come around in time. Yet, if she thinks she'll convince anyone else, then she's a greater fool than I imagined."

Basina got up from her seat. The smile on her face grew. "I never thought much of her to begin with. If she were the intellectual she claims to be, she'd have married that rich guy her father set her up with and ignored the ranting's of a dead mother. Look where it'll get her now."

Justus sighed, watching Basina's antics. Kalista infuriated him, by trying to push her beliefs on him. Yet, he did see something in her he couldn't explain that was different. And though he didn't want to admit it, he wondered if she'd found something better than what he and Basina had.

Kalista's Hope

***

Chapter 22

Terentius nodded to the stone mason, his eyes lighting on words drawn across a heavy, rounded tomb marker. "It's exactly the way I want it."

He peered out the window onto the street and spotted a small red-haired child, free-spirited and barefoot in the grass next to her house, chasing after her older brother, laughing with delight.

A painful expression flitted across his face, and he spoke again softly. "Take care of it quickly." He closed his eyes. "It's the least I can do."

The man shook his head, heeding his words. "I will."

Terentius left the shop, turning from the child and taking urgent steps in the direction of his home. He planned to leave for Pompeii in two weeks time, and yet everything needed to be in place first, ready for his daughter's return.

***

"What did you do with them, Terentius?" Domnica hissed at him. Her black eyes struck him with venom as she shot past, her white stola trimmed in dark blue whipping behind her in a fury. "Venus is gone. The golden casket, too. And I can't find the serpent or any of the other Lares anywhere."

Terentius got up from a wooden bench in the garden at the center of the house and placed his hands on his hips. "They're gone, Domnica. We've no use for them here. I've removed them all."

He stared at the large goldfish swimming in the pond and waited for the explosion he knew was coming.

"I didn't believe it! They told me, but I thought it wasn't true! You can't be serious, Terentius! Why?" She stormed over to him, defiant.

He got up and laid a hand on her arm. "Now, Domnica, I can explain."

She yanked her arm away as if burned and took a step back, her cheeks red with angst. "Explain? This is Rome. We need those gods. Our lives depend on them." She gripped the folds of her silk gown and looked up at him, her eyes black as night. "I want them back."

Kalista's Hope

He knew what he said next would throw her into a boiling rage, but figured it was better to say it now and get it over with. "But, Christian homes don't have Roman gods." He planted his feet solidly on the tiled walk between the rows of flowers and faced her determined.

"Terentius?" Her eyes narrowed and looked like daggers pitted against him. Her mouth was grim and quiet.

Terentius tried to take her hand. "Come…" His lip curved slightly.

"No." She shook her head.

"I was with Gaius, and he helped me understand it."

"The lawyer's a Christian? By the gods, Terentius! What did he say to you? How could he do this?" She tapped her fingers against the edge of gown, slanting her dark eyes at him warily.

"It's simple, Domnica. I can tell you what he said."

"No!" She shrieked. "I don't want it! Do you hear me? I just want my gods back!" The kohl lining her eyes, began to run at the angry tears streaking her cheeks. She brushed them away and pursed her lips, unable to speak.

"I am head of the home, and you'll listen to me. They're useless, bitter poison to us now." Terentius looked over at one of the statues in the garden. He rolled his eyes. Could he ever get away from them? How many were there in Rome?

"You can't take them from me! Where will I pray or offer sacrifices?" She looked at him in desperation.

"Domnica…"

"Give them back, Terentius! Or I'll tell the Roman officials!"

He stalked across the room and held her by both arms. "You'll do no such thing. If you ruin me, you'll ruin yourself. Those gods have no life in them. They're wood and stone, fashioned by human hands. They can't see or hear or understand anyone. But, if you feel you must, you can give your sacrifices to them, outside this home."

"I'll sacrifice to them in here! I don't care what you say, and you'll lose everything, if you don't listen to me. They'll take you away, and everything you have will be mine!"

She lifted her fists to his chest and tried to pummel him with them, but he caught her arms and held them firmly at her side, despite her struggles to free herself.

137

Kara S. McKenzie

"Not when Kalista is listed as the next successor to all my properties. You'll want me alive." He let go, and she backed away.

Domnica halted in her tracks, and her tears suddenly stopped. Her face ignited with a twisted hatred. "Kalista?"

"My daughter."

"You're mad!" She drew her face to his, studying his expression. "But, she's dead."

"No. I've had news that she's very much alive in Pompeii with Justus."

Domnica's eyes drew wide. "But...they told us, the slaves?"

"No. She wasn't in the collapse, and she's listed to inherit almost everything of mine." He met her eyes boldly with his own. It's done, and it's all you need to know."

Domnica stared at him, as if she'd opened a grave and stepped in. She put her hand to her throat bewildered. "But, you don't care about her?"

He sighed. "You're wrong. I've always cared for her. I just didn't know it, until now. And I didn't want to accept what I felt in my heart."

Domnica withered under his stare. "But, I'm your wife? You wouldn't do this to me."

Terentius shook his head. He made his way to the arched stone entrance in the room and lifted the curtain to enter the atrium, holding it there while he regarded her warily. "I have, and it's for your good. You'll be cared for. Now, this conversation's finished."

He ducked under the filmy cloth and left Domnica glowering open mouthed behind him.

***

Chapter 23

Camila tapped her fingers against the folds of her tunic as she stood waiting for Nona to make purchases at the market. The heat of the day beat down upon her, and she wiped back the damp tresses against her forehead, letting out a breath.

She wished she'd stayed home, as she hadn't seen anyone of consequence since they left. She wanted to parade her new jewels in front of one of her high-ranking friends, but nothing seemed to be working for her this day. She fingered the emerald stone necklace set in a heavy, golden frame in the shape of a bird that swung from a chain around her neck and then she muttered under her breath. "Why's Nona taking so long?"

Two children ran past her, chasing each other and giggling, their togas sweeping the streets, as they zigzagged across the path.

Camila let out a sound and put her hands out to stop them from running into her. She had no patience for children and just wanted this day to end.

The loud street sounds around her, made her want to retreat to her room in the house again. People shouted from behind their seller stands bartering with customers, sometimes angry when they weren't getting what they wanted. Their high-pitched screeches echoed in Camila's ears, while the buzz of laughter and wagon wheels rolling past, added to the bothersome sounds.

She wondered where Nona disappeared to, as she looked across the street to a fruit stand under a tent.

Her eyes stopped to rest on a tall, attractive man talking to the vendor. He reached out and petted the side of a mill donkey attached to a cart next to him and laughed at something the vendor was saying.

There was something familiar about the man, but she couldn't quite be sure if she'd seen him before. She studied his features more closely. His dark-blue eyes sparkled beneath blonde hair that tumbled over his ears in a disheveled sort of way. She watched him, smiling at the vendor, and thought how his magnetic grin could surely charm many a woman.

She drew back. Her hand went to her chest, and a look of recognition flitted over her face when she realized where she'd last seen him, outside the gates of Janus only weeks before. He was the one she'd seen speaking to Kalista.

She watched him, wondering what he might have wanted with her wretched stepsister. The likes of Kalista would surely hold no appeal in this man's eyes.

Camila reached up and checked to see if her hairpiece was secure. She pinched her cheeks, a crooked smile making its way across her face.

Zipor, one of the family slaves, was standing next to her. She touched his arm. "Zip, tell Nona I'm just across the street. Stay here. I need to speak to that man." She pointed to the fruit stand.

Zipor nodded.

Camila walked across the street, eying the man curiously. She made her way to the table, sideling up next to him. Baskets filled with fruit were in rows on a wooden table in front of her. A sly look crept over her face. She reached for a pineapple on the other side of the man, bumping his arm. "Oh, excuse me, sir." She smiled. "I hope I didn't disturb you."

He backed away from her. His tone was steady. "You did no harm. Don't worry."

"Well, I couldn't resist the beautiful fruit."

She reached out again and took hold of a pineapple from one of the baskets and set it in front of the vendor. "Here." She handed the man a couple coins. She cradled the fruit in her arm, with a self-satisfied grin.

The vendor behind the table looked pleased. "Thank you, miss."

Her reply was short. "Yes." All the while she eyed the younger man next to her with open admiration.

She put her hand on the mill donkey's fur next to him, despite the fact it disgusted her to touch the dirty animal. Men usually liked a woman who showed care for animals. "He's on holiday today." She batted her eyes at him.

"Yes, the poor donkey's having to bear these absurd decorations." He gave the animal another pat and smiled. "The ninth of Junius."

Camila leaned closer to him and sniffed at the garland and bread loaves encircling the donkey's neck. "It smells divine." Her nose crinkled distastefully, but she smiled as if she liked it.

"Yes. Vesta's festival. I'm sure the sad little guy will be pawing to get back to work tomorrow."

Kalista's Hope

Camila pulled on a strand of her hair and didn't say anything. She tried to give him a seductive look.

"I only know how I'd feel, if I were this pitiful creature with bread loaves pinned to my side." He smiled.

"I believe he *will* want to go to work, because of that." She laughed, her kohl-lined eyes slanting up at him.

"Yes." He eyed her cautiously then turned to the vendor. "Well, I suppose I must be on my way, Otho. I've clients to attend. Let me know if you need me again." He paid for his wares.

"I'll see you, Gaius." The vendor pocketed his money and smiled. "Enjoy the rest of your day."

Gaius tipped his head to Camila. "Miss."

"It's, Camila." She gave him a sly look, and then frowned when he disregarded it.

As he started to walk away from the stand, she called out to him. "Sir!" She tugged on his arm and sidled up to him again. "I think I know you from somewhere."

He pulled away. "I'm sorry, but I really must be on my way. I'm meeting someone soon."

"But, I believe I saw my stepsister speaking with you outside the gates of Janus? Kalista? And your, Gaius?"

He turned round, suddenly interested. "Kallie? She's your stepsister? Have you heard from her?"

She made a face. "Kallie?"

"My name for her." He smiled.

"I suppose it fits. A little less cultivated." Her brows shot up.

He laughed. "Yes, well. She wouldn't like to be considered cultivated, anyway." He slung a bag of things he'd purchased at the stand over his shoulder. "So, did your father learn anything else about her?"

She looked annoyed, shaking her head. "Well, no…she left, and I'm sure won't be back. I heard that man call your name, and realized you were the one who knew my sister."

He studied her face. "Yes, and I spoke with your father just last week about Kallie, and the will of course. Has he heard anything?"

Her lips turned down. "Oh, you're the lawyer."

"Yes." He nodded, moving aside as a cart wheeled past, carrying lumber.

141

"You, do understand our household was turned upside down after you left. Now, father's half mad, and everything's in a mess. Mother won't even talk to him." She gave him a disconcerted look.

"I'm sorry. Your father was distraught and asked questions. I only told him what I knew."

"Which changed everything. My father's changed. He doesn't seem to care about the money anymore and smashed all the household gods."

"There's a reason, Camila." He looked as if he wanted to tell her something else, but was silent.

"Nothing I'd consider for our good."

"But, it is. It may seem mad to you for smashing the gods, but your father truly has peace now, something he never had before."

The interested expression on her face vanished and was replaced with a scowl. "Can you not repeat the drivel that's ruined everything. I'm going to lose my rightful inheritance because of you."

"But, the inheritance was Kallie's to begin with, not yours."

"It would've been mine if you hadn't of interfered!" Her fist tightened, her cheeks reddening.

Gaius eyes softened. "I'm truly sorry for your difficulties. You father plans to care for you, also."

Camila made a face. She turned when Nona waved to her from across the street.

"Mistress!"

Then she looked back at Gaius, and her ire lessoned when she saw the sincere look on his face. "My slaves are finished. And I need to go."

"I'm sorry, Camila. I never wanted to cause you trouble."

She sniffed. "Well, you definitely have thrown our household into an uproar."

He touched her shoulder. "I hope things will eventually be better for all of you."

She pulled away and set off across the street to where Nona and Zipor waited with baskets of fruits and vegetables in their arms.

Camila looked back at Gaius. *He* was the lawyer. What bad fortune she had. He looked like the handsome god of war, Ares, with his broad shoulders and noble features. She stared

142

Kalista's Hope

down her nose coldly, lamenting on the fact that his foolish religion spoiled everything. She understood why Kalista ran away from him.

***

Chapter 24

Camila stared at the view through the dining room window. The city of Rome spread out in massive proportions and covered the valley between the hills where they lived. The strong gates around the city and enormous, solid wooden homes stretched as far as the eye could see and seemed to be invincible. The wealthy people in the city such as herself, possessed about everything they could have wished for in this place.

Camila seemed to hold the world at her fingertips, and possess more than most women could dream possible. So, why lately, did she feel lacking?

She sighed. She bought so much in the marketplace, extravagant gowns, lavish jewelry, exotic perfumes and the latest oils and creams, and yet it was odd that those things never seemed to satisfy her cravings for more. Sometimes it seemed a vicious cycle, one she couldn't stop. She never felt as if she had enough.

She looked around the room. All the chairs were empty and only a couple slaves stood waiting by the door. Her mother was in the forum today, and Camila had no clue where her father had gone. His behavior was so odd lately, she didn't know what to think of it. She was sick with the thought that he'd gotten rid of all their household gods and was turning the household into mad chaos.

He tried to talk to her about his new faith, and she wanted to please him. But the Christian faith? This is what he wanted her to embrace?

Whenever she thought of it, it made her skin crawl. She couldn't imagine living the prudish life these people lived. It wouldn't be any fun, from what she saw. She'd be a slave to following their ways, and she'd be stuck going to their stuffy meetings. Why would anyone wish for such a thing?

She took a sip of wine and put the container back on the table. Did he understand what he was asking of her? Did he know what she'd be giving up?

Some of the things he told her, made her feel very afraid. Especially when he talked of the afterlife and where she'd be if she didn't change her life. She knew she wasn't perfect, but didn't want to hear what the consequences would be for the

Kalista's Hope

wrong things she'd done in her life, unless she repented. She shuddered at the thought.

She wrestled with her feelings. As odd as her father's behavior was, there was something Camila saw in him she'd never seen before, and liked. Could she be happy, living in this new way?

It was a puzzle to her. He was so different, now. He hated Christians before. How could he accept them so readily now? And he used to be constantly scowling and accusing everyone, or trying to goad her mother into a fight. But now, his expression was calm, and even held a hint of humor in it. He even seemed content. In his eyes there was a soft, gentle look, the same one she'd seen in Gaius. She couldn't understand it.

She drummed her fingers against the table. She didn't like the thoughts she'd been having lately. Maybe, if she went somewhere, she could push them from her mind and forget about all of them.

Where was her mother? Why had she left without her?

Camila got up and called for Zipor. "Get my wrap. I need to leave this home, or I'm going to go crazy."

Zipor grabbed the fabric folded over one of the chairs and came rushing to her, handing her a dark blue one.

She took it and pulled it around her tightly, her eyes wild. "Please, Zip. You must take me somewhere in the city to relieve my mind from bothersome things, somewhere where I can have fun."

Zippor nodded. "To the games, miss? How does that sound?

Camilla motioned to the door. "I suppose it'll be all right. Maybe I'll quit thinking about the mess our house is in now. It hasn't been a good day."

***

145

Chapter 25

"She knew my mother?" Kalista leaned across the table. She fixed her eyes on her aunt.

Cyra nodded. "They were good friends."

Kalista cupped her hand over her open mouth and sat in stunned silence. Then she dropped her hand and fiddled with the folds of her tunic. "And she lives in Rome?"

"Yes, but quite a distance from your father's home. It's too bad you never knew her."

"But, no one ever said anything?" Kalista could understand her stepmother keeping the information from her, but her father? She shoved a strand of hair behind her. Why didn't he tell her that her mother's friend lived in Rome? She fumed silently. There was so much left unsaid, too many things she should've known.

Her aunt took her hand. "Your father wanted no reminders, Kalista. He was in such distress. And of course, Domnica wanted the relationship to end."

"But, it's not right. They could've said something." She blurted it out, angrily. She put her hand in her lap, shaking her head. "It wasn't right." It grated her inside for not being able to control the resentment brewing in her, and she wondered if she could ever forgive her father for the things he did.

Her aunt didn't say anything, but got up from chair she was reclining on and went to the window. She looked out. "He loved her, Kalista. If you could've known him then, you might understand."

"But, why couldn't *he* love *me*!" Kalista burst out in the heat of her anger. "What did I ever do?" She shoved back a tear pooling up in the corner of her eye. "He couldn't even love his own child?"

She got up and went to the door, fumbling with the latch on it.

But, before she could get it open, her aunt was at her side and took her by the shoulders. "He loved you. He did. He just didn't know how to let *her* go."

Kalista felt a rush of hot tears and tried to hold them back, struggling to keep her pain within her, but instead she lost control of it, and something in her broke.

Kalista's Hope

Maybe it was her aunt's gentle manner and conviction in her words, or the soft touch of a hand on her, but she couldn't stop the tears and couldn't hold herself together any longer.

She turned and fell into her aunt's embrace, the rush of tears spilling onto her cheeks. "Oh, Aunt! It's just too much." She felt as if she were suffocating. "He doesn't know what he's done. And I just don't know how I can ever forgive him." She looked pained. "Oh, what a Christian I've turned out to be."

Her aunt held tightly to her, smoothing out the length of her hair. "No, Kalista. You've learned to fight." Her voice held a tinge of mirth in it, but also one of seriousness. "But, now you'll need to learn how to love. And God can help you, if you just keep putting your trust in him."

Kalista lifted the folds of her tunic to her face, mopping up the tears. She bristled at the thought of loving any of her family at this moment and wondered if she'd ever want to. But, she took heart in her aunt's words to heart. Maybe someday, it was possible. "If that ever happens, I'd be surprised. But, who knows? I didn't think I'd ever be a Christian, either."

Her aunt smiled. "And you are."

Kalista was suddenly serious. She took her aunt's hands in her own.

"Yes?" Her aunt tipped her head, her eyes curious.

Kalista took a breath. "I'd like to meet the friend. If I could talk to her, she might be able to tell me things. You say you remember little of my mother, because she left Pompeii when she was young. But, this woman, she'd have known her."

Her aunt touched her arm, holding her hand. "I was going to wait to tell you. But since it's already arranged, I suppose it'll be all right." She smiled. "You'll be taking a trip to Rome with your uncle in the next few days. It just so happens he has business to attend north of here. You can talk to your mother's friend then."

Kalista's eyes widened. "Really?" She looked directly into her aunt's eyes, as if for confirmation.

Her aunt nodded. "Yes. You'll see her."

Kalista lifted her hands to her and clasped them together. She laughed. "Oh, my. I could burst right now from the excitement! You're so good to me! I don't know what to say!"

Then, she went to the door and opened it, laughing and shouting outside. "My God has done so much for me!"

147

Kara S. McKenzie

Her aunt pulled her back inside. She was lit with excitement and chastising at the same time.

"Kalista! You mustn't be so bold. Don't you know the Christians are not so popular at this time? Please, hold that tongue of yours." Though serious, her eyes were sparkling. "My! What have we done, teaching you this?"

Kalista let out a whoop, then, shouted again, twirling about the room. Without watching where she was going, she tripped over the chair and tore the corner of her tunic, as she slipped to the floor.

When she got up, she was chagrined as she held her hand to her dress. "I'm so sorry, Aunt. I didn't mean to tear it. Really, I didn't."

Her aunt laughed again, her eyes merry. "I just hope we can get you back in one piece to Rome. If we do, it'll truly be something to marvel at."

Kalista shook her head. "Well, at least uncle's patient with me. He just might be able to do it." But, inside she wondered at what a daunting task it was, keeping her from difficulties. Her aunt didn't even know the truth of it.

***

Chapter 26

"I'll pay you well to hunt her down and find her."
Domnica handed a bag of coins to the seedy looking man standing
next to her. "You'll get the rest when you've done what I asked."

"What does she look like?" He fingered the pouch
greedily. "And I'll need a name." He gave her a sidelong glance,
as he chewed on his scraggly beard.

"Her name's Kalista. You can't miss her with that bright,
red hair. It's never combed and is usually loose down her back.
Her eyes are light brown, and she's small, but sturdy. She'll be
wearing upper class clothing, yet you'd hardly know it, with all
the tears and smudges of dirt in them.

The man rubbed his whiskered chin. He growled, "So,
what do you want me to do with her when I find her?"

"What do you think? Why else would've I come to you?"
She scowled. "Kill her of course. But, make sure there's proof of
her death. And find her before her father's servants do."

His right eye cracked slightly open. And then he grinned.
"Consider it done."

Domnica lifted her hand to his face and smiled. Her nails
rubbed against his cheek. "See to it, and I'll pay you generously."

He looked annoyed. "Yes, well, I'll be back for the rest of
the coins, very soon." He wiped his sweaty palms on the side of
his leg. "And you'll have what you want, sooner than that."

Domnica watched him find his way to the door. She
looked furtively around. If anyone discovered what she was up
to, it would ruin everything. But, if all went as planned, the
whole household would one day be hers, and she wouldn't have to
answer to anyone, ever again.

***

Chapter 27

"I'm tired of this shabby castle with its drafty halls." Nero's expression was that of a demanding child.

Poppaea patted his arm. "But, why? We've everything the way we like it. And I've spent so much time with the décor. What will I do without all the slaves, if they're busy working on a new palace?"

Nero stopped pacing. There was a wild look in his eye. He reached for her. His fingers clenched tightly around her slender arm. "I'm not asking. It's already decided. And if I have to bring more Greek slaves into the city to do it, or make slaves of any Christians I don't kill first, the project *will* be finished."

Poppaea pulled away and rubbed her arm. She arched a brow at him. "But, I like it here. We've settled in. It's all decorated to my own tastes. I don't see why…"

Nero rubbed his throat, and his eyes set upon her like a hawk. "Stop!"

She started to talk, then hesitated and took a step back, nervously flipping her hair over her shoulder. "I didn't mean…"

His lips curled back, and he suddenly pounced upon her, throwing her up against the wall, his hands around her throat like a vice. "I told you to stop! And you never listen!"

She choked and gagged, trying to free herself from him, as he held her tightly there.

His eyes were rolling back, showing only the whites of them. He shoved back hair that had fallen in his face and shook his head.

He pushed harder against her, as she coughed and gagged again. And then he leaned closer and murmured in her ear, a smile on his face, his grip tightening on her throat. "You know, I could end your life right now, and no one would know."

Poppaea didn't move. Her eyes were like marble, as she gurgled out of her mouth, sucking in as much air as she could.

He had a speculative grin on his face, as he held her there. And as suddenly as he'd grabbed her, he let her go and watched her crumple to the floor.

He began to laugh, stumbling about the room, a hysterical look in his eye.

Kalista's Hope

Poppaea got up and backed away, holding her neck. She didn't speak, but watched him nervously.

Nero went to her and took her in his arms, fingering her blonde plaits hanging over her shoulder and then touched her bruised neck. "You're my sweet." He whispered it to her, chuckling as he said it. "But don't forget, who got you where you are."

***

Chapter 28

Kalista stepped onto the street in the early morning. As Rome awoke, the forum filled with vendors and politicians. The marble paving stones beneath her feet were so much easier to walk on, than some roads in the city. It was a promising day, as her uncle planned to take her to her mother's friend's home later. She looked forward to finally talking to someone who could give her a clear picture of who her mother was.

They'd arrived late the previous evening and settled into her uncle's friend's home for the night. This morning, she had some time to spare and decided to look around the street.

Men set up tents and put out choice fruits, breads and fish on mats. Others sold brightly colored fabrics and spices from the orients. She fingered a green cloth that was soft to the touch, smoothing out the crumples in her own blue tunic. The streets were full of the life of the city, and her heart danced within her at what the day would bring.

***

Gaius was up early and made his way through the streets. He'd left home to meet with Kalista's father and strode through the forum, stopping for a brief moment to purchase a jar of wine at a stand to take back to the Neo household. He reached for a tall slender container at a stand and then heard his name from behind.

"Gaius!"

It was Camila.

"You're visiting my father today?" She called sweetly to him.

Gaius turned, eying her warily. Camila was on her way toward him through the crowded forum. Her blonde hair was swept up behind her in a fashionably braided knot, and her expression was coy. Although she was a pretty girl, he thought she could do without so much make-up. The dark lines beneath her eyes and heavily rouged cheeks hardened her face. "I'm going there later. Yes."

She came closer. "Can I walk back with you?"

"I might be a while." He turned to pay the vendor for the wine.

Kalista's Hope

Camila looked nonplussed. "Oh, come now." She placed her arm in his and smiled. "I need an escort." She quickly gave him a peck on the cheek.

Gaius frowned, but she tugged harder, pulling him along.

She began to giggle, lowering her eyes and pushing a strand of hair off her face.

He wasn't buying her antics, yet he shrugged and threw her a reluctant smile. "Fine. We'll go there now. I do need to talk to your father."

***

Kalista drew back into the shadows watching her stepsister from across the street. The back of her throat constricted, and something inside her churned, after witnessing the exchange between Camila and Gaius. It was obvious a relationship had developed between them. And Gaius didn't refuse her.

She sighed. But, it was the way with her sister. With her seductive smile and willowy looks, dressed in the latest form-fitting fashions, how could he not fall for her charms?

At this point, Kalista knew Gaius and her were through. Camila always found a way to get what she wanted, and it was obvious what her devious stepsister had her heart set on.

***

Kalista hesitated at the door before she knocked. She looked back at her uncle who sat on a cart watching her. He nodded as if assuring her to go forward with her decision.

She turned back to the door of the quaint, rectangular villa and made two quick raps and then held her breath. She wondered what her mother's friend looked like and if she'd remember much about the past. Her heart raced with the thought of the meeting. She couldn't imagine the stories she might hear.

There was a sound of footsteps behind the door and then a lift of a latch. A tall, dark slave in a white robe greeted Kalista. He tipped his head. "And who might you be?"

"My mother was once a good friend of your mistress. I was hoping to speak with her." She stood in the doorway, anxious to see the woman.

He looked somewhat chagrined. "She's busy and is at the moment overseeing the spinning of wool. I don't think she'll be able to come to the door."

Kalista looked pained. She'd traveled so far and waited so long. She wanted so much to meet this woman. "Could you

153

please tell her my mother's name? I think she'd be interested to know."

He sighed and looked at the back room. "I'll try, but can't promise you anything. What is it?"

She turned to see her uncle still waiting at the cart. "Gabriella Neo."

He bowed slightly. "I'll tell her, and then will let you know what she says. Please stay."

Kalista cleared her throat. "Thank you. And let her know, my name is Kalista."

He nodded and turned, leaving her standing inside the door.

She called to her uncle. "Wait for me a little longer."

He waved at her. "Don't worry. I'll be here."

She smiled, a lump forming in her throat. She was jittery inside as to what the woman's answer would be, and she knew she'd be devastated if she had to wait another day to see her mother's friend.

She turned and looked around the great hall. The walls were decorated with ancestral portraits of the family on the wooden walls. There was, a warm inviting feeling in the room, very different from the home she'd grown up in. The tall, white columns she stood between at the doorway rose up like a gated entrance next to her.

She tapped her fingers against her gown.

"Kalista?"

The curtains of a side door opened, and a statuesque woman in a dark, blue toga entered. There was a light in the woman's eyes, and Kalista couldn't help admiring the thick blonde hair that fell over her shoulder like a wave.

Kalista looked out the door again. "I'll find my way to your place later, uncle! She's here. I need time."

Her uncle nodded. He chucked the reins, and his donkey moved down the road, clomping lightly over the cobblestone streets, leaving Kalista back at the house with her mother's friend.

Kalista struggled to talk, but didn't know what to say, so she fell silent.

The woman just stared for a moment, as if she were seeing a ghost. Then, she composed herself. "I'm Sandra Sergius."

She took Kalista's hand. "Gabriella's daughter. My…I realized it was true, the moment I saw you."

154

Kalista's Hope

Kalista searched Sandra's eyes, uncertain. "You did?"

"Yes."

Kalista trembled. "I saw a painting, but I didn't think I looked like it. No one talked about her in our home."

Sandra was full of compassion. "I'm sorry. It must have been difficult." She couldn't seem to take her eyes from Kalista. "It does not feel real that you're here. I've so much to say to you."

Instantly, a warmth encircled Kalista, and she immediately liked Sandra. Not only was the woman hospitable and kind, it was apparent she cared deeply for her mother at one time. She might finally have some questions answered.

Sandra motioned for them to go into another room. "Come, let's go to the garden to talk. The sun is out. Let's not stand in the hallway."

Kalista followed Sandra past an office and into the Peristylium where they took a seat near a carved fountain in the center of the garden.

She tried to sit straight-backed and tuck her feet up under her tunic. She'd been worried about what to wear that morning. The light, blue gown her aunt made for her, complimented her auburn hair, which she pinned behind her, with only a few loose coils managing to escape.

Sandra smoothed out the white stola she wore over her tunic. Kalista noticed the aquamarine jewels edging her gown and sandals and the round gold amulet swinging from her neck.

Though Sandra's wealth was not equal to her father's, Kalista could tell she lived quite comfortably. Kalista wasn't surprised they'd never crossed paths, as this home was on a hill far from hers. And yet, she wondered why Sandra had never spoke to her before this.

"How come I never knew you?" Kalista wondered aloud. "You were my mother's good friend, and you never said anything?" She watched Sandra closely.

Sandra turned and looked at the fountain in the corner of their garden where a small pond of water with fish in it was. She didn't say anything at first, reluctant. But then she spoke softly. "I thought you were…"

She paused and then began again. "Domnica told me that both you and your mother died. She said your father was too distraught to have anyone associated with your mother near him.

155

I was told to keep my distance. And our with our homes being at far ends of Rome, I never knew you existed."

Kalista's eyes narrowed and she let out a breath. "Ooh. Domnica. I should have known she had something to do with it. Father rarely spoke to me about anything." Something raw touched her inside.

"He was hurting. And I'm sure never quite got over your mother." She shifted in her seat, drawing the stola around her shoulders. "But, it was wrong to take it out on you."

Kalista shrugged, resigned. "Yet, if it weren't for me, my mother wouldn't have died. And she was so perfect, so good."

Sandra reached out her hand and took Kalista's again. "Kalista, it was never your fault, and your mother would never have blamed you. But, she was human. And no one is perfect."

"But, I know she was really good, because for my father to love her the way he did, she had to be." Kalista bristled slightly. She felt the heat rise to her face and got up to pace the stone tiles.

"She was sweet and kind, but wouldn't have wanted you to idolize her." She smiled. "It's why I think your father loved her so dearly was because of her ability to tell him just what she thought. He used to laugh when her cheeks turned bright red, just like yours."

"My mother?" Kalista was astonished. She couldn't imagine her mother having had a temper.

"You didn't know much about her, did you?"

"Nothing. I found out what she looked like from an old fresco on a wall, which wasn't very clear. We weren't allowed to talk about her in my home. No one told me anything." Kalista sat back down.

"I'm sure you reminded your father of her, especially your hair. So much of you, from what I see, resembles your mother."

"I didn't know this." Her whole life, Kalista drew upon the little things she learned about her mother, like the words on the tombstone. She never guessed the image she'd conjured up, might not be accurate.

They both looked up when a young slave girl came to them, smoothing out her tunic. She stopped in front of them and bowed. "Would you like anything? The other slaves told me to come and ask."

Sandra motioned for her to go back. "No thank you, Julia. We've important matters to discuss."

156

Kalista's Hope

The girl nodded and bowed again. "I'll tell them." When she saw the look on both of their faces, intent on getting back to their conversation, she disappeared quickly through the arched door and into the other room.

Sandra spoke quietly. "And then he married Domnica." She looked sad.

"Nothing like my mother." Kalista knew this to be true, but wanted to hear it firsthand.

Sandra was quick to respond. She looked out over the garden grounds, her eyes lighting on a patch of white flowers on the path. "No, I believed Domnica was after your father's money. He never saw it, at least at first. But, we all thought this. The only similarity, I saw between your mother and her, was that both of them were able to speak their minds to him."

Kalista was quiet. She knew Domnica was very different from her mother, otherwise her father would've been a much different person, like the one who wrote the words on the tombstone.

"Your mother was beautiful, inside and out. She cared for others, and when she stood up to someone, it was usually in defense of someone else."

Sandra smiled. "Our slave girl, Julia, was one of them." She looked out the doorway to the garden.

Kalista didn't say anything.

"Of course, Julia was a baby at the time. But, your mother refused to allow her to go to another family. She wanted Julia to remain with her mother, a slave at their home, who was distraught at the thought of losing her child. Your mother wouldn't back down to your father."

Kalista smiled. This was the mother she'd always imagined. "Did you have children at the time? Did she know them?" She wondered about Sandra's friendship with her mother.

"We've four, two girls and two boys, but they're all grown. Maximus was just a baby when she was alive. But, the others I had afterward. She loved Maximus, and he loved her."

Kalista smiled. "I knew she would've been like that." Something told her, her mother would have loved children.

Sandra nodded. "And your father loved her for it, too."

Kalista's dark eyes were solemn. She pushed a strand of hair out of her face. "But, not me."

"I'm sure he was afraid to love again."

157

Kara S. McKenzie

"Maybe. But, most likely he blamed me more for her death." Her eyes hardened, and she toughened herself inside. "It's all right, though. I didn't need him."

"Oh, no." Sandra reached out and clasped Kalista's hands. "You needed them both, and you had no one."

Kalista didn't respond.

Sandra's eyes grew soft looking, and she sighed. "I loved your mother, and I see her in you. So, I can't help but feel something very special when I met you."

Kalista lifted her chin. "Really?" It surprised her, this woman, along with her aunt and uncle, could show such affection. It was foreign to her, but she was beginning to like it.

Sandra smiled. "Yes, I wish I would've known you sooner. I would've cared for you."

Kalista's eyes misted over. "At least, we know each other now." She looked down at her sandaled feet.

Sandra shook her head. "Yes. And I'll do my best to answer any questions you have about her."

"I'd be grateful for it." Kalista's eyes shone. She wanted to know everything she could about her mother from the time Sandra first met her. There were so many pieces to her life she didn't understand and now had the opportunity to know.

They spent the good part of an hour talking about the past. Kalista's heart lifted, as she heard more about the life her mother and father led before her death. She felt as if she understood her father a little better from the things Sandra told her. She'd only known him as a hard, detached man with little feeling, and wondered what he might have been like, if things hadn't happened the way they had. She realized that she'd also adopted some of his traits, not having had a parent who showed warmth toward her. Knowing his struggles helped her to feel something inside for him she'd never felt before.

She noticed the shadow on the sundial giving indication that the day was getting late. She needed to be getting back. She pointed to it. "I suppose I should be going. Our time went fast."

Sandra nodded. "Oh, I didn't know it was so late. I need to get back to work, too. I have to get done, so I can have a little extra time. I've been compiling some poetry, for a book I'm making."

"You write poetry?"

"I do. Maybe someday you can read them."

Kalista sighed. "I'd love to."

158

Kalista's Hope

"But, that will have to be another day."

"Yes." Kalista got up. A couple long strands of hair had fallen from the pearl clasp in her hair. She pushed them over her shoulder. She began to talk, but was interrupted by a sound from outside the door of the garden.

"Mother, the servants want you in the sewing room."

Kalista recognized the voice and turned to the doorway. Her mouth opened slightly.

It was Gaius. She remembered the last time she saw him, arm in arm with her stepsister. What was it he said? Mother? Sandra was his mother? How could this be?

He entered the room. The look on his face was one of surprise. "Kallie, what are you doing here?"

Sandra looked interested. "You know each other?" She scrutinized both of their faces.

Gaius strode down the path toward them. He looked from his mother to Kalista. "I was going to ask you the same thing?"

Kalista let out a breath, annoyed that he could ruin a time she felt had been so special. She ignored the way he was staring at her. All she could think of was her stepsister strolling down the street at his side.

Sandra took her son's arm. "I knew Kalista's mother, but didn't know they had a daughter. I told Kalista things I knew about Gabriella when she was alive."

Gaius blue eyes sparked to life. His smile was genuine. "Really? That's wonderful."

He let go of his mother and moved closer to Kalista. His expression was tender. "We've a family connection. I'm glad my mother was a help to you. But, Kallie, what are you doing in Rome? And what's happened to you since we've last seen each other?"

Kalista didn't answer. It infuriated her that he seemed so interested, after he'd just spent time with Camila.

Sandra smiled. "I need to go now. Unfortunately, I must get back to work." She leaned over and gave Kalista a hug. "I wish you well, dear. Come visit when you can."

"I will. You don't know how glad I am to have met you." Despite her being Gaius' mother, Kalista knew she'd find her way back here someday and spend more time with the woman.

After Sandra left, Kalista turned to leave. She wanted nothing more to do with Gaius, after seeing him with Camila. She lost any trust she had in him and didn't want it back.

159

"Not so fast." Gaius took her by the shoulders.

She sprung back from his touch, her cheeks hot coals. "I can't stay. I've a lot to do." She gave him a look that would wither the strongest weed.

He laughed. "So, I see, you haven't changed, have you?"

Her eyes narrowed. "Not in regards to you."

He blocked her path from leaving. "But, I want to know what you've been up to. When you've told me everything, then you can go."

Kalista turned slightly and looked over at the fountain in the middle of the garden. She tried to move past him, but he blocked her way. She backed away bristling. "I see you'll not let me alone, unless I tell you what you want to know."

He kept his stance, crossing his arms in front of him. "You might as well tell me now."

She gave him a resigned look. "All right, if you must know. I found my aunt and uncle in Pompeii. They took me in, and they told me about your mother. Of course, I didn't know it was your mother. They were surprised I hadn't met her. So, I came back here."

"Naturally. But, what happened to Justus? Your husband?" He took her arm to stop her from pacing. His blue eyes sparkled.

She snapped at him, her eyes flashing. "You knew very well we weren't married."

She backed away from him annoyed by the way he made her feel when he was close to her. "He's probably married now…to a loud-mouthed girl with money. Basina. But, if it's what he wants, I guess there's not a whole lot anyone can do about it."

Gaius' expression grew serious. "I missed you."

She turned slightly, looking at the tiles beneath her feet. Something inside, made her want to respond to him in a like manner and tell him how much her own heart longed to see him. But, she couldn't help thinking of him and Camila walking arm in arm and instantly drew back.

"Kallie."

"Please, I can't stay. And don't try to follow me. I don't want to see you anymore." She felt a lump forming in her throat, and her heart raced.

She could read the disappointment in his eyes, but left him, practically flying out of the room and down the hall. She

Kalista's Hope

wanted to run back to him, but couldn't get past the idea that he had for even a moment, considered her stepsister. No, she mustn't trust him to love her the way she wanted.

She made her way through the front doorway and onto the path that led away from the house, and noticed he didn't follow.

***

Chapter 29

Kalista's uncle's home in Rome was comfortable and to her taste. It was less extravagant than anything she'd ever lived in, yet it suited her. Despite the home having less rooms and little in the way of décor, the walls reminded her of her own bedroom, which she loved so much. The frescos were covered in lively colors with simple designs of birds. The look was warm and quaint.

Her uncle was at the forum today conducting business, and she was left to her own devices at the house. She was stretched out on a long, wooden bench on a set of pillows in the garden room, enjoying the warmth of the summer sun.

After relaxing for a while, she turned when a commotion in one of the inner rooms broke out. She got up to investigate, but drew back when her father came in through the doorway, one of her uncle's slaves following nervously at his heels. She dropped into a low bow, her heart racing at the thought of what might become of her. How did he know she was here?

Terentius Neo frowned at the servant behind him. He waved his hand at the young girl. "I only want to speak with my daughter. Leave us."

Kalista called to the girl. "Do as he says. It's all right." Her heart practically stopped at the thought of being left alone with her father, but knew she wouldn't be able to stop him.

The young servant looked relieved. She backed away and disappeared around the corner without a word, leaving Kalista to deal with her father alone.

Kalista didn't lift her head from the floor. Her mind was racing in all different directions. Her heart wouldn't slow in its beat, and her breaths were short. She heard her father's sandals heavy against the hard floor.

"Get off the floor." His voice was an order.

Kalista obeyed immediately, standing in front of him, her eyes downcast. "Father, I can explain." She wasn't able to hide the edge to her voice. Someone told him about her whereabouts. Gaius was the only one who knew. He'd hear about this.

Terentius lifted her chin with his hand, so that their eyes met. She noticed he had a wild look in his eyes, yet they were

Kalista's Hope

softer than she'd ever remembered seeing and were filled with moisture.

She was puzzled by his expression. "Father?" Why was he acting like this? What did it mean? She'd never seen anything but icy glares from her father, and now, he looked as if he were pained. There was a gentle expression in his eyes. It wasn't the father she knew.

He choked on his words. "I thought I'd never see you again." He lifted his hand to her hair and brushed it back from her face, staring at her as if seeing her for the first time.

Kalista's mouth opened slightly, and she drew back, wondering at the change in him. This was the only time in her life he'd ever showed her any emotion other than anger. She was stunned by his broken expression.

He touched her face and then put his hand at his side. "God gave me a second chance. He answered my prayers."

"Father?" She said it again in disbelief. Was he speaking of the household gods? She wondered why he kept staring at her, as if he were seeing a past remnant. It felt odd and unreal.

Then, he reached out and held her to him in a tight embrace, and she heard a sob escape him. Even when she tried to pull back, he wouldn't let her go. He held her there for what seemed a long time. "Gabriella's daughter. You're so much like her." He spoke in a whisper.

At those words, Kalista felt tears begin to well up in her own eyes. She couldn't believe what she was hearing. Her mouth opened slightly, and she drew in a breath.

"She told me to be good to you, but I didn't listen." His voice broke. "I wanted you to hurt as much as I hurt, but it wasn't right. I'm sorry."

Kalista wiped the tears back from her face. She loosed herself from his grasp and looked at him. She sensed something different in him. She felt peace in his presence. She knew the reason for the change. "You're a Christian?"

He nodded.

She'd never seen him smile before, but he did, and it seemed almost unreal to her. Her father, or the one she'd known all her life, was not the same.

"I read a letter from mother that my aunt and uncle gave me. And I'm a believer, too." She watched his reaction.

163

Kara S. McKenzie

His eyes misted over with tears, and he choked on his words. "I'm glad for it. I wish I would've been a better father to you."

"I always loved you." Tears formed in her eyes again.

He hugged her to him another time. "Things will be different between us from now on."

She wondered if she would ever see him differently. It seemed strange to her and not real. But, she knew it was.

They spent the better part of the afternoon telling each other about their lives and what happened to them after Kalista left home. Her father filled her in on how he met Gaius and on what their conversations had been.

Kalista couldn't imagine what Domnica thought when she found no household gods in their home anymore and the rage she might have displayed. She knew it was wrong, but would have loved to be there to see the look on that woman's face, when it all happened.

They shared their thoughts about Gabriella and how much she meant to both of them. If it weren't for her mother writing the note, or Gaius sharing his faith, neither might've found the peace they both desired. They resolved that nothing would ever come between them and their new faith.

"Father?"

"Yes?"

"I'm going to stay with uncle for now. But, I'll be home, soon." She sighed. "I want to learn more about her side of the family."

He patted her shoulder. "Take the time you need. I'll wait."

"It won't be long." She smiled. "There'll be changes soon, though."

He laughed. "There already is."

When her father finally left, Kalista sunk down on a soft chair and clasped her hands in front of her. She dreamily looked around the room, feeling like the birds in the paintings, free spirited and full of song. There was nothing she wanted more than what she'd experienced in her room that day. It was the end to a perfect day.

***

Chapter 30

The next morning, Kalista spoke with her uncle and learned the news of what Camila had done to her former slaves.

She knew what she was going to do wasn't right. Her uncle warned her against it, but she didn't care. Camila had to pay for selling Tasia and Chaya to Nero.

First, Gaius, and now them. She'd had enough and was going to visit her stepsister and let her know what she thought. She'd make Camila get those women back from that crazed emperor, if she had to march her to the palace herself.

***

"She's Christian?" Gaius looked stunned. "And she never told me?"

Terentius laid a hand on his shoulder. "I don't know why, but I'm sure she had her reasons."

Gaius sighed. "I thought she'd be happier to see me, but was so cold this time." He shook his head. "Maybe she was still mad at me for turning down her proposal."

Terentius seemed amused. "Proposal?"

Gaius sputtered. "To get out of marrying Barbatus. She made it clear this was her reason."

Terentius laughed. "Sorry, but, it seems she has a little of me in her, aside from her mother. But, at least you share beliefs." He had a twinkle in his eye.

Gaius shook his head back and forth, then smiled. "I suppose I've my work cut out for me. But, you're right. We can agree on this one thing."

"She's at her uncle's house. I've some business to attend to in the forum, but can send for someone to take you there."

"I'd appreciate that." At least Terentius was on his side and was willing to help.

Terentius reached out and took Gaius' hand to shake it. "I'll say prayers for you."

Gaius laughed. "Thanks. I'll need it." He turned to head out the doorway, anxious to be on his way.

***

Camila spent the better part of the morning shopping in the forum. She hadn't run across Gaius as she'd planned and was wondering where he was. She knew the places where she could usually find him, but he wasn't at any of them.

She half-heartedly fingered the silky emerald fabric beneath her fingertips and motioned for the cloth seller to come closer. "How much?" Lately, she felt as if her time spent on the street gave her little satisfaction. There seemed nothing new to add to what she already had.

The stout, dark-haired merchant reached out a jeweled hand and rubbed the cloth between his fingers. His one eye narrowed as he looked at her. "One libra."

She made a sound, but reached into her drawstring purse and pulled out the amount, handing it to him and taking the fabric in her hand.

He looked satisfied, as he slipped the money into a small, wooden box.

Now, where to? Camila thought. She snapped to her slaves and pointed down the street. "Come. We've more shopping to do." She handed the fabric to Ariston and turned to leave.

She looked down the street. Maybe spending the rest of the day in the forum would brighten her spirits. She wasn't sure what else there was to do.

***

Kalista moved quickly through the streets of Rome on the way to her father's home to clear matters up with Camila in regards to her slaves. As her she made her way down the cobblestone streets, past temples, people in prayer before gods, street vendors and Roman soldiers casually strolling past, she caught a movement behind her. Someone was following close behind.

She didn't recognize the whiskered man at her heels, but was quite certain he'd been there since she left her uncle's home. She turned around to confront him. He was dressed in a dirty ragged tunic, belted with a leather strap. His beard was long and scruffy, and he walked with a limp.

"What're you doing?" She didn't like the way he seemed coiled like a snake, ready to strike.

The man squinted one eye, his face hardening. He moved closer, a low growl in his throat. He looked down the street, then back at her, and his hand went to his belt. He took a small dagger from it, holding it in his hand in a deadly grip. He barked an order. "Don't move. I won't hurt you."

166

Kalista's Hope

Kalista didn't believe him. She quickly realized his intentions and jumped backward as his hand flashed, and he took a stab at her. Her eyes narrowed, but she didn't turn from him. She called out to the crowd. "He has a dagger!"

She wanted others to see what he planned to do and wasn't going to wait for him to make another move before they did.

People around them stopped, some immediately leaving. Others formed a circle around her and him. One of the men in the group yelled at the scruffy man. "Put it down! Leave the girl alone!"

Kalista backed away, lifting her gown so she didn't trip. Although her heart was heavily pounding in her chest, she managed to further the distance between them.

He let out a snort, eying the bystanders watching. "She tried to swipe my money pouch! She's a thief!" He raised his dirty fist in the air and shook it at her.

Kalista was incredulous. She couldn't believe the audacity of the man.

"Liar!" She shouted back, looking at the crowd. "I didn't touch you or your money bag. Why would I, when I have plenty? You've been following me since I left my uncle's place! And I'd like to know what the reason is."

Her eyes narrowed, and she stood her ground.

The man wiped the sweat from his forehead and squirmed. "She's a beggar, I tell you!" He put the dagger back in his belt and began to back away.

"Beggar! Terentius Neo's daughter? You think I'd care for your worthless coins?" She pointed at him as one with authority, despite her rumpled clothing and fiery hair spilling out over her shoulders wildly. "Ask my father. I'll take you to court! You don't knife a defenseless person."

The people in the circle rallied to her cause, and began nodding and shouting.

He scowled at her, until he realized he was at the losing end of the argument and shook his head. "I was sure of it. But, might've been wrong."

Kalista glared at him.

He lifted his robed arm and waved the crowd off. "Aw...I made a mistake, all right." He put his knife away. "Fine. You win. I was wrong." Then he turned and slunk off into an alley next to the circle of people.

167

Kara S. McKenzie

She watched the place where he disappeared, as the crowds dispersed. Her expression was hard. She wondered at the man's obvious lie and attempt at her life. Only one person came to her mind, as to who could have put him up to it. Domnica.

She'd have to take care from now on to keep an eye out for any suspicious behavior. She looked around her. When there no sign of the man, she continued on her way.

***

Camila ran to her room and threw herself on her bed. She pulled her knees up to her chest and began to sob. She'd had it in the forum today after running into Corvina again. Nothing ever happened the way she wanted it to. Corvina treated her like a servant and could care less about her as a friend. Even those who mattered to her, her supposed friends weren't really friends.

And her father was right. She was cold as stone and treated everyone around her like the dirt under her feet. She was going to that place called Hell, and she would burn in an eternal fiery pit if she didn't do something about it.

So, what was it her father had said? That God would forgive her if she'd only repent and believe? But, would he really do this for someone like her? Wasn't she beyond help at this point?

Her heart quickened its beat, and she felt as if she couldn't breathe. The words her father told her kept pounding incessantly in her head. She felt something akin to fear inside her, and it was like a dark shadow chasing her and trying to tear her to pieces. She had to do something soon or she'd go crazy. She couldn't take it any longer.

She wrapped the covers on the bed tight around her. Her breath came in gulps. She seemed as if she were to the point of no return.

Maybe it was time to let go and give in to what she knew was right, time to believe in something bigger than herself, and listen to her father.

***

Kalista stormed past the household servants, who looked shocked, as if they were seeing a ghost. She heard them murmur to themselves as she went down the hallway to where she thought Camila might be. She was going to get to the bottom of this, and Camila was going to get Tasia and Chaya back.

Kalista's Hope

Domnica was in the central office of the home, writing on a wax tablet with a stylus. She looked up when she heard a commotion in the doorway.

Kalista swept into the room, eyes ablaze. "Where is she?"

Domnica eyed her curiously, a smile tugging at the corners of her lips. "Kalista. How good to see you."

Kalista's eyes were like ice. She ignored Domnica's greeting. "Where's Camila? I have to talk to her."

"How am I supposed to know? Not that it's any of your business." Domnica ran her hands along her desk, lifting her chin higher. She turned to the slaves in the doorway standing behind Kalista. "Leave us, as we've matters to discuss." She directed a poisonous stare at Kalista.

Kalista took a step closer. "Camila had no right to sell my slaves, and I want them back." She wrung her hands, watching Domnica's every move, not wholly comfortable being alone in the room with her.

"From Nero?" Domnica threw back her head and laughed. "You try it, and you're likely to become one of his wives for the day."

Kalista's eyes glittered. "Those slaves were mine, and now they're suffering at the hands of that monster because of her." She wanted to reach out and wring Domnica's thin neck. All the rage of the past seemed to be surging up inside of her.

Domnica frowned. "You were supposedly dead, so she had every right to do with them whatever she wanted. But, that's beside the point. I've other matters, much more important to discuss with you."

She took a scroll from a vase and pulled it out, thrusting it at Kalista. "Sign it."

Kalista narrowed her eyes. She pushed the document away with her hand. "Whatever it is, I want nothing to do with it. I'd rather die, than sign something you gave me."

The room was menacingly silent, and there was an acrid odor. It was as if Kalista could smell Domnica's red, hot anger. The walls even seemed to broil around them. She supposed it might be one of the lanterns set out around the house.

Domnica flew across the space between them and grabbed Kalista by the shoulders, knocking her off balance. A vase on the small table fell down and shattered against the tile floor. Domnica grabbed a shard of thick pottery and held to Kalista's throat. "Maybe that's what it will take."

169

Kara S. McKenzie

Kalista didn't move, but spoke in a hushed tone, the burning smell more intense. She looked up and saw smoke, but ignored it. "That man was sent by you, wasn't he? To kill me?"

Domnica eyed her dangerously. "It would've been easier that way." She tightened her grip on the flat end of the shard.

Kalista quickly shifted, pushing Domnica to the side. She tried to break Domnica's hold, while the two of them struggled on the hard, tiled floor. Kalista clawed at Dominica's face. "It doesn't have to be this way. You can talk to father."

"I want no more of his nonsense," Domnica snarled. "He's always favored you, as much as he tried to show he didn't. And I'm tired of seeing your obstinate, selfish face around here."

Kalista fended off another jab. She pushed Domnica's arm back.

Domnica's face turned to stone. "You won't get away so easily. I've been waiting for this for a long time." She got ahold of the shard again and smiled, victoriously.

"But, father will know. He'll find out."

Domnica lifted her arm to smash the shard downward at Kalista's chest when they both turned to sounds coming from the hallway, footsteps drawing nearer.

Shouts rang out in the house, and the thump of sandaled feet passed the doorway in the hall. Slaves ran down the hall. There was a loud explosion and something heavy falling. A scream rang out in the corridor.

Kalista wondered what was happening. Clearly, whatever it was, it affected the whole household.

At that moment, Gaius shoved his way into the room behind Domnica and pulled her from the floor. He grabbed her wrist and squeezed it until she dropped the sharp piece of pottery. "Stop this. We have to get out of here." He pointed to the doorway. "The city is burning! Everyone's saying Nero set it on fire."

Kalista backed away from him, not knowing what to say.

Domnica looked dumbfounded. "It isn't true. It can't be happening."

He pushed Domnica aside and watched as she ran out the doorway.

Kalista got up, her face flushed. "You came for Camila?" Her hair fell precariously over her shoulders, the knot on the back of her head coming loose. Chalk from the shard, dusted her cheeks.

170

Kalista's Hope

He shook his head, his face registering surprise. "I came to warn your family. I was kind to her, because she's your sister. Kallie, I'm not interested in her."

She looked at him, incredulous.

"But," he said. "We have to get out of here." He took her hand and pulled her in the direction of the doorway. Flames were lapping at the wooden sections of the structure and curling around the walls.

The smell of smoke was strong, and it left a caustic taste in Kalista's mouth. She covered her face with the sleeve of her tunic and allowed herself to be led through the scorched marble hallways and onto the street.

Her eyes widened, as she looked across the city. Black smoke was roiling over the tops of the homes as far as she could see. People were running and screaming, huddled with family members, looking for carts to ride out of the city on.

She heard a caterwauling screech behind her and turned to see Domnica on the roof, flames on all sides. She was clutching the edge of the building and crying as if half mad.

Gaius shouted over the fray. "Wait. I'll get her."

"No!" Kalista shrieked. "Gaius! Come back!" She reached for him, but he was already a step ahead of her, charging back toward the home. She fell on her knees in terror, watching him go, praying for his safety.

As he neared the building, there was a crashing sound, and the outer walls came tumbling down on top of him, pinning him under it.

"Gaius!" She screamed and ran to him, crouching on the cobblestones beside him. He was unresponsive.

Tears stained Kalista's cheeks, as she tried to pull him free, the flames down the street closing in on them.

A horrifying wail came from the top of the roof, and Kalista looked up to see Domnica engulfed in flames, her gnarled hands reaching out to possess the walls of the house, which collapsed inward, taking her with it.

Kalista strained as hard as she could, to get the stone that was pinning Gaius' shoulder to the ground, off him. She was sobbing and crying for help.

One man stopped and tried to push the large chunk of marble off, but to no avail and then took her hand. "You can do nothing for him. You must save yourself."

171

Kara S. McKenzie

"No!" She wailed. "Please!" She tried to pry herself loose from the man, but couldn't. She was being dragged down the street, watching as the flames swept through the city toward Gaius. Her heart felt as if it were being torn from her chest.

***

Chapter 31

Nero sat on a hill far from the city, watching Rome burn. He took up his lute and began to play, singing a mad song, a smile forming on his lips. "My golden city, my golden jewel built on the backs of men. I'll have it again, a bigger one, have it the way I want it, built on the backs of men…" he crooned. Every now and then he took a sip of wine, periodically stopping to press the flask to his head.

He filled the container, and a twisted grin formed on his face. "They're saying I started the fires and am the cause of all the mayhem. Do you think it's true my sweet, Poppaea?"

Poppaea shuddered, pulling her golden wrap across her chest. Her face was contorted and eyes slanted. "If you did…it's your city. And you can do what you want with it."

He threw his head back and laughed, an unhinged sound, taking his lute back up into his hands. He began to strum. "My city…and I can do what I want…" he sung with a crazed look in his eye. "…and I can do what I want…"

***

Chaya and Tasia banged on the walls of inner room of the castle. How much longer they could stay in this place, they didn't know. Smoke began creeping into the lower room where they were locked. They clung to each other unable to believe this could possibly be the end for them.

They screamed until they were hoarse.

They prayed for anyone left to discover them and set them free.

But, they didn't hear anything from outside their silent tomb. It was only a matter of time before the fire engulfed the darkened space.

***

Kalista was thrust onto the cart and taken out of the city. As the wheels jolted along, bouncing over the smoke-filled path, past blackened Roman gods and out of the city, Kalista felt the chasm between her and Gaius grow. She pictured him on the street beneath the flames, unable to move. The thought of his end, being anything near to what she'd seen Domnica endure, was devastating to think about. She covered her eyes and wept. She was sure she'd never see him again.

Kara S. McKenzie

***

"The floor!" Tasia whispered, her eyes burning from the smoke. "Do you hear it?"

Chaya crawled closer and listened to small tapping sounds. She nodded, finding a trap door in one of the corners.

The tapping sound became more insistent. "It must lead to the aqueducts. Someone's down there!"

Tasia's eyes lit with the possibility of freedom from the room that had become their prison. "I hear them."

They both moved back, when the metal door beneath them begin to move.

It opened and a slave appeared in the space below them. "I knew you had to be close." It was Antonius. "I found others, but wasn't sure which one led to your quarters. I'll get you both out."

They struggled to get through the trap door, but finally managed, dropping into a workman's tunnel and onto a pathway filled with rushing water that flowed through huge, cavernous corridors, underneath the city. An aqueduct propelled them out of the smoky cell above them and down a path toward freedom.

***

Chapter 32

A few days later, as evening approached, Kalista found herself back on the streets, dazed and confused among the smoldering ruins, searching for any sign of Gaius. She stood silent and watchful as she eyed bodies being placed on carts and taken out of the city. There was a numb feeling inside her too desolate to comprehend.

She heard no word from either Gaius, or her father. The city was charred and black, the incessant smoke sent bitter spirals of dust up into the air. The people around her wandered aimlessly about, searching for lost ones, the pain in their faces deep.

She sat down on the side of the street, regretting the way she'd coldly brushed Gaius aside at his mother's house. Did he understand she'd cared for him? Was it possible he knew this? If there were any chance he were still alive, would he ever forgive her for leaving him to die on the streets alone?

She rubbed the tears that fell from her eyes with blackened fingers, making smudged stains on her cheekbones. Her hair was wild and loose over her shoulders. She shoved it behind her. She was tired, having slept little in the past few nights.

She struggled to right herself and walk through the shadowed, acrid streets one more time. She found herself on a cobblestone path headed toward her mother's grave. It was the only place she might find comfort.

***

Chaya stood in the middle of the street, her eyes trained on the path in front of her. She lifted her arm to wave one last time to Antonius and Tasia who were on a cart headed toward Greece, the homeland they'd been torn so violently from.

Tasia held Antonius' arm, tears dropping down her cheeks as the wagon rumbled quietly down the street, away from the city and from the friend she'd grown to love.

Then, Chaya dropped her arm to her side, as the cart disappeared into the distance.

Few slaves had been recaptured. Chaos still ruled the streets, and the Romans were more interested at this time in locating loved ones they'd been separated from during the fire and searching the ruins to see what they could salvage from their

Kara S. McKenzie

homes, than chasing down the hundreds of lost slaves they could find later.

Chaya wasn't sure what she'd do now, alone and unprotected on the streets. She hadn't found anyone going in the direction of her parent's home, and wasn't sure if it was even safe to do so. She was relieved it was still daytime.

She rounded the corner of a burned, charred building. Paying little attention to where she was going, she slammed into a man of considerable height, jarring her backward and forcing her to the dusty street.

One of such stature could only be a Roman soldier, and she cringed at the thought. "I'm sorry." She rose from the cobblestones and bowed low, her hair falling into her face.

"Chaya?" A low voice uttered in astonishment. A hand came to her side, lifting her up.

She drew back from the mention of her name, looking at him, fully expecting it to be one of Nero's household workers, or worse yet, one of Nero's friends. But, she was struck by the fact that it wasn't. Instead, the sandy haired man in front of her was Atticus, his blue eyes fixed on her. "It's you." It's all she could manage to say.

Atticus breathed a welcome sigh. "Finally. You don't know how long I've waited for this." He reached out and took her in his arms.

The feeling of warmth and love surrounded Chaya, and she spilled tears of joy. He'd come for her and hadn't forgotten. She was no longer a slave to Rome, but able to leave this city.

"I knew you would keep looking."

Atticus smiled, drawing back from her. "I had to believe you were still alive. The night you disappeared, the story your sister told didn't make any sense. You had no reason to go out, as I'd seen you safely inside that evening."

She nodded. "I'm so glad you never believed it."

"I am, too." He breathed a sigh of relief. "And now, I'll be able to get you out of here. With this fire, it'll be easier with so much confusion."

Chaya smiled in agreement with him.

Then, Atticus turned slightly, as if realizing there was something he was forgetting. "Pardon. I'm sorry. I should've said, but I've someone with me, you should meet."

176

Kalista's Hope

Chaya looked around. "Oh." She quickly moved away from him, her cheeks growing warm at the thought of someone else seeing her in such close contact with him.

Atticus motioned to a woman standing behind him.

A scarlet-haired woman with a bright flowing tunic stepped forward, a white stola draped over her shoulder. Jewels to match her clothing, adorned her wrists and neck.

Chaya wondered at the familiarity Atticus and the woman shared. There was a bit of reservation in her eyes.

"Chaya, this is Jocheved."

Jocheved smiled and nodded, a smattering of freckles over the bridge of her nose practically dancing as she spoke. "Hello, Chaya." Her expression held a hint of devilment, as if she knew the admission she was about to give would relieve Chaya. Her eyes sparkled as she spoke. "I'm Atticus' sister."

Chaya turned to Atticus, her eyes wide. "Your sister?"

Atticus put his hand on Chaya's arm. "The musical one I told you about, who taught me the lute. She helped me search for you here."

Chaya reached out and took Jocheved's hands in hers. "I'm so happy to meet you. Atticus has told me about you." She eyed the tapestry Jocheved held in her arms.

Jocheved lifted it up. "It took some time, but I wanted something to give you when we met. I've been working on it in Rome, and it will be yours upon our return."

Chaya eyed the intricate designs stitched lovingly into the pieces of brightly colored fabric of purple, gold and turquoise. Being a seamstress herself, she smiled at the work gone into the piece. "I'd be honored to have it."

Atticus took her hand in his. "So, you'll be coming with us?"

Chaya smiled. "I don't think you need to ask." And then she sighed. "But, you should know. I'm one of Nero's slaves. You're risking a lot to take me out of the city."

Atticus grinned. "I figured as much, so not to worry. I've a cart, and Jocheved has a set of clothes for you. We've a long ride. Come."

***

Kalista couldn't believe what she was reading on her mother's tomb. The inscription and stone she'd read for years had vanished, and another had taken its place. She read it again, in case she'd been mistaken.

177

Kara S. McKenzie

'To release Gabriella, our darling,
to the heavens this day,
Was toughest price for us to pay.
In death her jeweled eyes will light our path,
And her delightful smile will gentle our earthly wrath...
My dearest sweet bequeathed a gift that night,
A cherished, flaming babe to rekindle light,
And with this gift, Gabriella is set free,
Entrusted with a peace, bestowed upon by Thee.'

Kalista's father's words struck her hard, and she knew his pain had been as deep as her own. The comforting words on the stone assured her that she was loved, and that her father wanted her and the world to see it.

She began to weep. The words on the inscription were so full of forgiveness and so difficult to comprehend. She wanted to cling to the idea, like she clung to her new faith.

Her father loved her and had changed the inscription to let her know.

She cherished the moment, not quite believing all the changes in her life and how they'd come to be. Everything she wanted had been handed to her in a brief moment of time, wrapped around her heart like a thick, warm stola on a chilly winter's day. She finally knew what it felt like to be cherished and held dear by the ones who mattered most to her. Her mother would surely look down and be pleased.

As she sat next to the stone, fingering the etchings lovingly, the crisp night air stole in around her, and she shivered. She looked across the expanse of the city and watched tendrils of smoke slipping high into the blue sky, painting streaks of ash over the horizon. She pulled her hand from the gravestone, her fingers grazing the rough, scratchy surface.

Her father was gone, and so was Gaius. What was she going to do? She'd had no contact with her aunt and uncle and wasn't sure where to look for them. She was alone. There was no one, and she was left to fend for herself in this charred skeleton of a city called Rome.

Despite, the feelings she'd experienced when she read the tomb, she suddenly felt very afraid, without a soul to turn to. She wrapped her arms around her shoulders and rocked in place, trying to console herself, something she'd done as a child to quell the sick feelings inside.

Kalista's Hope

She put her hand to her chest and then wiped a lone tear from her cheek.

Kalista felt scorched by the sadness tearing at her heart. Rome was blackened by dust and charred on the outside, but she on the other hand, in the core of her being, was smoldering with the ashes of despair and branded on the inside. Rome would be restored. But, she wouldn't. Nothing could repair the emptiness she felt.

She picked herself up and out of habit, headed for Janus.

***

Chapter 33

Kalista walked through the gates of Janus and made her way to the front of the statue. She looked up at it, eying the two-headed figure staring off in opposite directions. What she was doing here? She didn't know?

Her life wasn't the same. This god wasn't going to offer her any protection. Or any of the other gods in the city.

She sat at the base of the statue. She had time to think on the way from her mother's tomb. Gaius and her mother were right. The God of the universe was different, like no other. He accepted her as a friend when she opened her heart to him, and filled her with his presence. Everything was changed! Everything was new!

When she prayed at her aunt and uncle's home, she'd felt an indescribable peace inside, one she could not begin to understand. And she'd seen this in her father and Gaius, also. The God of the universe had become as real to her as her own father, and her trust was no longer in herself, but in him. Things that controlled her and bound her before, had little effect on her now.

He was a loving and sovereign God, one who cared for people, even in the midst of tragedy. He held the world in his hands and touched lives in ways that most could not even comprehend.

She sighed and clasped her hands in front of her, knowing there were still things she didn't understand.

As she sat at the base of the statue alone, having lost so much, she wondered to herself how a God so powerful and so good, who cared so deeply for his people, could allow such suffering? Her life had been filled with so many tragedies? And she didn't understand the purpose?

And yet, it was through these difficult times, she'd come to know him. She wouldn't have understood how great his peace and love were, without having known the suffering. And surely, her painful journey, had brought her closer to him. She felt the full effect of his love and his forgiving heart, by knowing what it was like to be devoid of it.

She wished she could be so loving and forgiving as he had been toward her, though. On the day of the fire, she'd hated

Kalista's Hope

Camila for what her stepsister had done, selling off her slaves. She wanted to chastise her stepsister and then hand her over to Nero. And afterward, she'd watched Domnica perish in the flames, without even flinching. How could she be so cruel?

If only she could take back everything she said and did that hurt both Domnica and Camila. If only there were second chances. She hoped someday there would be, at least for her stepsister.

She turned away from Janus and looked up at the sky, breathing a quiet prayer. "Lord, let my hope be in you. And let me remember, that when I have nothing, I can trust in you."

She eyed the colors weaving paths of orange and gold across the great expanse of the universe and felt God's presence surrounding her and touching her heart. She wished to be like this heavenly Father, who loved her, even when she didn't deserve it.

She smiled with the hope welling up inside her. It was something no other religion afforded, a hope for good things to come.

"Why did I even think to come here?" She spoke aloud. "A god of sculpted marble, made with human hands, offers nothing. Where should I go?"

She heard a rustle and turned.

"You could look outside the gates."

Kalista's eyes locked onto Gaius' clear blue ones, and she practically flew across the courtyard and out under the arch. She flung herself into his arms. "You're alive! Oh, Gaius!" She held him tightly to her, as if she'd never let go.

She lost her balance and almost took him with her.

He caught her before she fell, smiling. "The doctor just let me go. Do you want to put me back there?"

For the briefest of times, she looked concerned, until she saw the sparkle in his eye, then she pushed on his chest and wagged a finger at him. "You know I don't."

He laughed, and then murmured in her ear, pulling her closer. "Kalista, your father would like to see you, also. And Camila."

She looked over Gaius shoulder and let out a squeal. She pushed him aside and ran to her father and stepsister. She hugged her father first, and then reached out and tenderly put her arms around Camila.

She felt a surge of happiness spread through her and lifted her eyes to the heavens. In this instance, God was allowing her a

181

second chance, and she fully intended to take it. In her eyes, the past was forgotten.

Camila was alone, left as an orphan without a mother. Kalista couldn't bear her stepsister experiencing an inkling of what she went through. "I'm so glad you're all right, and you got out."

Camila looked spent and solemn, yet a dim light showed in her eyes. She nodded and hugged Kalista back. Tears dropped down her cheeks. "Mother's gone."

Kalista's heart went out to her. "I know. I'm sorry." She held tightly to Camila's shoulders. "I'm sorry for everything."

She handed Camila over to her father, who put his arm around her. "Father will care for you."

Her father nodded. Then he pointed to a cart and mule. "We'll need to leave and go to the summer estate to live. Gaius is coming with us. We've been looking for you."

She turned to Gaius and took his hand in hers. "The city's destroyed. Our home's gone. There's nothing left for us here."

Gaius agreed. "My mother's already left to their country estate and knows I'm staying with Terentius."

Kalista looked relieved. "I'm glad your mother's all right. The city is a mess."

Kalista's father nodded. "Yes, and the longer this goes on, the more trouble there will be. I pity the people still here when Nero comes back."

Kalista shook her head. "This is true."

They made their way to the cart and got in. Camila, turned to Kalista and smiled. Her eyes were gentle.

Kalista smiled back. There would be changes. Life was never going to be the same for any of them. And yet, she knew right then, that there was hope in this hopeless world. The God of the universe would see to that. With Him, there would always be hope.

***

Chapter 34

"How many years has it been since we've seen Kalista?" Justus was standing in front of the fresco of her mother and father.

Basina snorted. "Hmph! I don't know. Years. Come, we have to get home. Why are you thinking of her right now? There's got to be something better to put your mind to."

Justus sighed. He wondered how Kalista fared in the fire that terrible day in Rome. He thought of what it may have been like for her and wondered if she had lived through it.

He walked out under the arch into the sunshine and was standing in the courtyard waiting for the slave to tie the donkey to the cart so him and his wife could get in.

A wave of guilt hit him, as he stood there in the open area. She might've died in that fire. If he would've taken her in, he could have spared her a tragic end. He winced.

Basina grabbed his shirt. "Come, we need to get going. Do you want to stand there all day looking like an idiot?"

He pulled his arm from her. "I can manage on my own." He gave her a rueful look and got up on the cart behind her.

He looked at the blue sky and thoughts came back to him of what Kalista had told him about God, so that he'd go to a place called heaven and be with her someday.

Through the years he'd wondered at the small changes he witnessed in her before she left town. He remembered how different she was.

The wagon rattled along, rolling through the countryside, closer to the heart of Pompeii and the base of the volcano where he and Basina lived. There were rumblings in the massive mountain, but nothing he hadn't heard before. He could even see a stream of smoke rolling out of the top. It was unusual, but only mildly interesting.

He grunted, much like the grumblings of his wife, sitting by his side.

For some reason, he couldn't get Kalista's face out of his mind this whole afternoon. It was as if she were beckoning to him, calling out, and he wondered what it meant. He heard her words, over and over pounding between his ears. Repent, and accept God. What could it mean?

He wished the constant thoughts would leave him. He was tired of hearing them, striking with force in the heart of him. He worried. Maybe, it was a sign?

He wasn't sure, but fearfulness suddenly overtook him, and he felt as if he couldn't breath. He looked up and saw a huge cloud had risen over the volcano. It was massive and stretched over the city, blackening the sun. Something wasn't right. The words came stronger.

"Basina!" He called to his wife. "Tell the slave to stop the cart! Now!"

Basina looked at him, as if he'd lost his mind. "What are you caterwauling about? We aren't even halfway home. And with that cloud, we'll need to get inside."

He reached out in front of him and took hold of the slave driving the cart and screamed at the man to stop.

Kalista's words were coming to him fast and strong now, like a drum, beating louder and harder.

The slave pulled on the reins and yelled, "Whoa!" He brought the wagon to a halt.

Justus jumped out and fell down. His heart continued to pound mercilessly, and his chest suddenly constricted. He yanked on Basina's arm until she nearly fell out of the cart. He pulled her onto the ground with him. "We have to repent! I know it! We have to accept Kalista's God, the God of the universe, before it's too late!"

Basina stood above him, her mouth gaping open, aghast.

"The cloud!" He yelled it, again. "We have to repent!"

He shuddered and dropped to the ground. He cried out. "I'm sorry for all I've done. Forgive me, Lord. Take me with you and let me be yours!"

Basina scowled and then suddenly lit into his side with her sandaled foot. "You imbecile! Get up. You're acting like a fool!"

The slave watched in horror, wondering if his master had lost his mind. He turned and ran, racing over the fields while Justus called to him to stop.

Justus coughed and sputtered and tears fell from his eyes. He lifted his face upward, and he cried out again, "Basina, please! Before it's too late!"

She got back onto the cart, her face defiant. "I'll not do that, you lambhead. That girl, Kalista fed you a bunch of lies."

184

Kalista's Hope

Justus screamed at her again, "But you have to! Please, Basina! Do it for me!"

She laughed a wicked laugh and turned away from him, grabbing the reins.

He kept screaming for her to listen, but she didn't.

She put her hand on the seat of the cart, ready to settle herself in. But, before she could sit down, clumps of volcanic ash fell from the sky and rained down from the blackened cloud over the mountain, sending instant ash and fire in all directions, freezing her in her spot.

Justus took one last look at her, before he was a cast in molten ash. No one in the city stood a chance. All were buried, destroyed in an instant.

***

Chapter 35

Kalista watched Gaius from where she sat in the garden room of the country home at her father's villa. Then she stared out the windows over the rolling fields below them. Grapevines hung over the lower wall that surrounded the estate. A cobblestone path meandered in a wavelike pattern over the grounds. It was hard to believe she was Gaius' wife and living in such a beautiful place in the country.

She shivered, thinking of Pompeii, her family's city, buried deep beneath the ash and molten lava. How quickly it must have been obliterated, in the blink of an eye.

"Do you think Justus might have stood a chance in Pompeii?" She eyed Gaius solemnly.

He turned to her. "You did what you could. You told him what you knew."

"But, do you think he listened?"

Gaius smiled. "God would've listened to your prayers. With him, there's always hope."

She leaned over and took Gaius' hand in her own. He was right. If God knew Justus would turn to him in need, he'd find a way to save her friend.

Gaius reached out with his other hand and touched her cheek, his eyes brimming with love.

Kalista looked north to where Rome was rebuilt. She shuddered, thinking of all the years of atrocities committed against people in the city. It was good to be Roman and living in a place where she could share her faith. God was keeping her safe, but she wondered for how long.

There would most definitely be difficult days ahead of them. Rome had changed, and Pompeii was gone. Her life as she'd known it was no more.

And yet, she smiled, feeling a glow inside, despite the uncertain future.

Gaius had faith. And with all God had given her, she felt she could brave whatever came her way. And with His promise of eternal life, she had nothing to fear. A fire inside her was lit, that would never go out.

***

Chapter 36

"Jonathan, what is it?" the woman asked. She wiped dirt from the side of her safari pants. She'd get another pair out of the jeep later and change in the tent.

The man whistled, low and quiet. "Something you wouldn't believe, Danielle." He lay down his tools and began ever so gently brushing aside the volcanic ash with his bare hands. The wall was strong and barely touched under layers of dust.

As they used their tools to uncover the colors beneath, a shadow of an image emerged.

Danielle turned her head sideways staring the fresco, her mouth open wide. "It's a woman. She's lovely."

She sat down next to it. "Do you know what it means? It's from when the volcano erupted, 79 AD. I'm sure of it. Honey, we've found a goldmine."

Jonathan sat down next to her and began to laugh. "You're right. She's beautiful. Look at the red hair and the clothing, right down to the earrings, so well preserved. Can you believe it?"

They got up from their seat and worked tirelessly until evening and then stood back, looking at their work. The painting was still faint upon the wall, but there was enough color to discern the smallest details.

Danielle touched the surface, ever so gingerly. "She's written a message using the stylus on the wax. I wonder what it says."

Jonathan shook his head. "It's anybody's guess. I suppose they were rich, judging from their clothing. What a beautiful couple."

"Yes." Danielle sighed. "It would be wonderful to know their story."

Jonathan took her hand. "I suppose only God knows that. And someday, once we've lived our life to the full, and have our own story, I'm sure he'll reveal theirs to us."

Danielle's eyes looked dreamy, as she studied the picture lovingly.

"Yes, I'm sure he will," she whispered. "And just maybe, he'll introduce them to us."

***

http://www.thecolefamily.com/italy/pompeii/slide25.htm

Their story is a mystery. Your guess is as good as mine.

Made in the USA
Charleston, SC
08 October 2015